P9-CBZ-727

"Sammy notices animals more than he notices people," Jack said.

Arianna looked up quickly. "That must be hard to deal with."

He nodded. "I'm used to it." He held up the puppy so Sammy could see it. "Dog," Jack said.

Sammy didn't speak.

"Does he know the word?"

"He used to," Jack said, and pain twisted his heart.

He met Arianna's eyes and saw a matching sorrow in hers.

The intimacy of their shared emotion felt too raw, and he looked away, focusing on the puppy. "He's healthy," he told her, "just too young to be left alone."

"Poor thing. I wonder what his story is."

Jack shook his head. "There are all kinds of reasons why a mother can't raise her pup," he said.

Arianna drew in a sharp breath, and when he looked up, her eyes glittered with unshed tears. Funny, he hadn't realized she was so sensitive. He put a hand on hers. "We'll find him a new mama," he reassured her.

She swallowed hard and nodded, and then Sammy started to fuss and the moment was over.

Lee Tobin McClain read *Gone with the Wind* in the third grade and has been a hopeless romantic ever since. When she's not writing angst-filled love stories with happy endings, she's getting inspiration from her church singles group, her gymnastics-obsessed teenage daughter, and her rescue dog and cat. In her day job, Lee gets to encourage aspiring romance writers in Seton Hill University's low-residency MFA program. Visit her at leetobinmcclain.com.

Books by Lee Tobin McClain

Love Inspired

Redemption Ranch

The Soldier's Redemption
The Twins' Family Christmas
The Nanny's Secret Baby

Rescue River

Engaged to the Single Mom
His Secret Child
Small-Town Nanny
The Soldier and the Single Mom
The Soldier's Secret Child
A Family for Easter

HQN Books

Safe Haven

Low Country Hero
Low Country Dreams

Visit the Author Profile page at Harlequin.com for more titles.

The Nanny's
Secret Baby

Lee Tobin McClain

If you purchased this book without a cover you should be aware
that this book is stolen property. It was reported as "unsold and
destroyed" to the publisher, and neither the author nor the
publisher has received any payment for this "stripped book."

LOVE INSPIRED BOOKS

Recycling programs
for this product may
not exist in your area.

ISBN-13: 978-1-335-47932-7

The Nanny's Secret Baby

Copyright © 2019 by Lee Tobin McClain

All rights reserved. Except for use in any review, the reproduction
or utilization of this work in whole or in part in any form by any
electronic, mechanical or other means, now known or hereafter
invented, including xerography, photocopying and recording, or in
any information storage or retrieval system, is forbidden without
the written permission of the editorial office, Love Inspired Books,
195 Broadway, New York, NY 10007 U.S.A.

This is a work of fiction. Names, characters, places and incidents are
either the product of the author's imagination or are used fictitiously, and
any resemblance to actual persons, living or dead, business establishments,
events or locales is entirely coincidental.

This edition published by arrangement with Love Inspired Books.

® and TM are trademarks of Love Inspired Books, used under license.
Trademarks indicated with ® are registered in the United States Patent
and Trademark Office, the Canadian Intellectual Property Office and in
other countries.

www.Harlequin.com

Printed in U.S.A.

Therefore if any man be in Christ,
he is a new creature: old things are
passed away; behold, all things are become new.
—*2 Corinthians* 5:17

This book is dedicated to all parents of children
with autism, especially my friend Laura,
who read parts of this manuscript to help me
portray the condition accurately.
All remaining mistakes are my own.

Chapter One

Jack DeMoise watched his eighteen-month-old son bang a block against the doctor's desk drawer.

"He's going to need as much attention and support as you can give him," Dr. Rutherford said. "We're learning more and more about this condition. His best odds would be to get a TSS—therapeutic support staff—team on board right away. Hope your wife is organized!"

Jack drew in a breath and let it out slowly before meeting the other man's eyes. "There's no reason you should remember this from the intake papers, but I'm a widower."

The doctor's face fell, just a little. Most people wouldn't even have noticed, but Jack was accustomed to reading emotions carefully, from small tells. It had been a crucial skill with his wife. "Do you work full-time yourself?" the doctor asked.

Jack nodded. "My job can be flexible, though." *Except when it isn't.* "I'm a small-town veterinarian. I've had several good babysitters, but I'm not sure any of them are up to…" He reached down and squeezed his son's shoulder. "To helping me manage Sammy's care the right way."

The doctor frowned. "You need someone experienced with kids, someone who connects well with him. Ideally, a person with special-needs experience, though that's not a requirement. A full-time nanny would be ideal."

And where was he supposed to find such a person in his small Colorado town?

The doctor stood and smiled down at Sammy. "Cute little guy. You can see the people in the front office to schedule his next appointment."

As the doctor left the exam room, Sammy lifted his arms, and Jack knelt to pick him up and held him close.

Autism.

The diagnosis didn't shock him—he'd had suspicions— but the reality of figuring out a coping strategy was hitting him hard.

Two hours later, back at their new home at Redemption Ranch, Jack had just gotten Sammy down for a nap when the sound of a loud, mufflerless car broke the mountain silence. He hurried to close Sammy's window, glanced back at the crib to make sure his son was still sleeping and then looked outside.

From this angle, all he could see was a tangle of red curls emerging from a rusty subcompact.

Arianna. He'd heard she was in town.

He took another deep breath before double-timing it down the steps to anticipate his former sister-in-law's loud knock on the door. Once Sammy was asleep, you didn't want to repeat the complicated process that had made it happen.

He opened the door just as Arianna was lifting her

hand to knock. Under her other arm, she held a giant painting, done in her trademark primitive style.

"When I heard you'd moved, I wanted to bring a housewarming gift," she said. "And a treat for Sammy. Sorry I didn't call first. Is this a bad time?"

"I just got him down," Jack said. He half felt like closing the door in Arianna's face, but he couldn't. She was his son's aunt after all, even if her chronic disorganization and flamboyance had driven his wife crazy, causing some disturbing family fights. Arianna was way out of his comfort zone. "Come on in," he said. "What are you doing in Colorado?"

She waved a hand. "I'm in town visiting family. Thinking about moving back to the area. Penny had mentioned she might do some art therapy with the vets, so I came up to try to sell myself."

"Out of a job again?" he asked as he carried the canvas she'd brought to the middle of the living room. "Pretty," he added, gesturing at the wild yellow painting.

"Jack!" She blew out a sigh he could hear from behind him and then flopped down onto the couch. "Yeah. I'm out of a job. How'd you know?"

He shrugged and sat on the big chair catty-corner to the couch. "Just a guess." He let his head rest against the back of the chair.

"You look awful," she said with her usual blunt honesty. "What's going on?"

He looked at her sideways without lifting his head. "Sammy and I visited the doctor today," he said.

She sat up straighter. "Bad news?"

"Yeah. No. I don't know." He kicked off his shoes and put his feet up on the ottoman. "We got a diagnosis I was hoping we wouldn't get."

"Oh no!" The panic in her voice was real. "Is he going to be okay? What's wrong?"

Her concern brought him upright, and he leaned forward, waving a hand to calm her. "He's fine, he's going to be just fine. It's not some horrible disease."

"Tell me!"

"It's autism."

She sucked in a breath, looked up at the ceiling. He thought she was looking in the direction of Sammy's room. Maybe even praying—she was a fairly new Christian, from what his wife had said only weeks before she'd died.

But when Arianna looked back at him, he realized her eyes were glittering with tears she was trying not to let fall.

"Hey," he said, moved by her concern. Everyone in town liked him and Sammy just fine, but there was nobody who felt the intensity of this diagnosis like he did. Or so he'd thought. "He'll be okay. It's just… I have to figure out how to cope, make some new plans."

"I'm sure." She drew in a couple of deep breaths and looked out the window. He wondered if the view of the Sangre de Cristo Mountains would calm her, like it did him.

"He'll be okay," he repeated. "There's so much help available these days."

"You don't sound that surprised." She studied him, head cocked to one side, eyes confused.

"I… No." He looked at her. "I kind of knew."

She frowned. "I *should* have guessed. I've done art therapy with kids who had the condition a fair amount, and now that you mention it…he does seem kinda like those kids. Although he's his own sweet, wonderful self," she added fiercely. "If he's going to grow up a little different from neurotypical kids, that's okay. I'll still love him just as much."

"I will, too," Jack said mildly, surprised at her vehemence. But on the few occasions she'd spent time with him and Sammy, she'd been an enthusiastic aunt. More enthusiastic about Sammy, when it came to it, than her sister, Chloe, his wife, had been. "The problem is that I have to hire a nanny, and there aren't many candidates in Esperanza Springs."

"I could do it," she said.

Jack stared at her. "You?" He couldn't keep the surprise and doubt out of his voice.

"Just until you find somebody permanent," she amended quickly. "I mean, no way could I do that long term, of course, but I'd like to help if you're in a spot."

"Wow, thanks, Arianna, but…" He trailed off.

How to tell Arianna that she looked too much like her sister? That she was too disorganized? That her liveliness and fun were a direct contrast to his own staid, boring life…and that they disturbed him?

She leaned forward, one eyebrow raised, a long leg crossed over the other. "What, Jack? Go ahead, say it."

"It's just… I guess I was thinking of a Mary Poppins type," he said, trying to make a joke of it. "You know, laced up and experienced and efficient."

"Sure. You're right, of course." She sighed and stood up. "I'm nobody's idea of a good employee apparently. But I'm here to help if you need me."

He felt like a heel as he followed her to the door, unable to keep his eyes off her chaotic, shining curls. "I appreciate your coming by and bringing the gift," he said, although truthfully, he had no idea where he'd put the giant sunflower. It didn't exactly match the couch. "Stop back and see Sammy anytime."

That comment made her whole form brighten, and she turned to him. "Thanks, I will. I miss seeing the little guy. I need a Sammy hug."

It occurred to him to wonder why she needed a hug, but that wasn't his business. He opened the door for her and held it while she walked out, the scent of musky roses tickling his nose.

Sometimes he wondered what it would be like to get involved with a woman like Arianna, colorful and warm and relaxed. But he always stifled the notion. He realized, almost instantly, that it shouldn't and wouldn't happen.

Love and marriage weren't about fun; they were about sacrifice and responsibility and hard work.

And getting drawn to Arianna made his face heat and his stomach churn with guilt, because of Chloe and all her suspicions. She'd died fourteen months ago, but her angry accusations still rang in his ears.

Anyway, and fortunately, no woman like Arianna would be attracted to a methodical, scientific nerd like him.

One minute later, his business phone buzzed, and five minutes after that, he was trying to figure out how to get someone to come watch Sammy while he drove to one of the neighboring ranches to help with a cow that was suffering from a dangerous case of bloat.

He'd moved from town up to Redemption Ranch because he'd seen how happy the wide-open spaces made Sammy. Made him, too, really. The fact that he believed in the ranch's mission as a haven for struggling veterans and senior dogs was a factor, too. Living here, he could serve as the ranch's on-site veterinarian, which was a needed role and one he relished.

On the downside, moving up here meant he was thirty minutes away from his normal babysitters, and they had both just refused to come at this short notice. He hated to impose by asking Penny, the ranch owner, or Willie, a Vietnam veteran and permanent resident of the ranch.

You could just ask Arianna.

The thought came to him, and before he could second-guess himself, he was out the door. Arianna was walking back toward her car from Penny's house. "She's not home," she called in explanation.

"Could you stay a couple of hours with Sammy now?" he asked, holding up his phone. "Vet emergency."

Her face lit up like he'd offered her the world. "Of course! I'd love to!"

He beckoned her in and showed her the laminated instruction sheets he'd made for Sammy's care. A little ridiculous, but Sammy was particular.

Now Jack knew at least a part of the reason why.

A smile tugged at the corner of Arianna's mouth. "It'll all be okay, Jack, really," she said. "I know Sammy, and I've worked with autistic kids before. Go help your… steer or whatever. We'll be fine."

Three hours later, Arianna patted Sammy's back as he bounced a bedraggled blue-and-white-checked bear. Whew. She'd finally found the toy he needed, and for the moment, he was content.

She, on the other hand, was anything but. Getting to take care of Sammy was sweet torture. She loved him with all her being, and Chloe had never let her be alone with him. She leaned forward and kissed the sweaty top of his head as he pushed his stuffed bear back and forth, humming tunelessly.

He glanced back at her as if slightly surprised but didn't reject the contact. Good. She knew that some kids on the spectrum resisted physical touch, but Sammy didn't seem to be in that category.

She looked around the living room, noting the bare walls, the end tables devoid of decoration, the shortage of pillows on the couch. Of course, Jack had just moved in. He hadn't had time to add the small touches that made a house a home.

Would he ever? Was he the kind of man who could do that, could be both mom and dad?

Oh, how she'd like to stay nearby and care for Sammy. But the job situation in the small ranching town of Esperanza Springs was bleak. At most, she might be able to cobble together some part-time gigs, but to support herself…not likely.

She'd find work aplenty in a bigger city, where her education would be valued and her references—which were actually stellar—could help her to get a job.

But she liked Esperanza Springs, had spent a lot of time here as a kid and young adult. Now, with her parents living in Europe and her sister gone, Sammy, plus the aunt and uncle she was staying with, were the only family she had.

And she was the only one who knew the truth about him.

The sound of a vehicle pulling in outside, the slam of a car door, made her jerk to attention. Was Jack back already?

Sammy held his bear to his chest and stared impassively at the door.

It opened.

It was Jack. And his handsome face went from gladness to amazed frustration as he looked around the living room.

Arianna looked around, too, wondering what his expression meant. As she took in the overturned basket of toys, the three sippy cups she'd tried until she'd found the one Sammy would accept, the box of diapers she'd brought down from Sammy's room and not found time to take back up, she realized what was bothering him.

"I meant to clean up," she said. Why was she so messy? When was she ever going to get organized? Chloe, thin and disciplined and neat, would never have let her house get into such disarray.

Of course, Chloe would never have let her care for Sammy at all.

"It's okay." He walked over to Sammy. He knelt beside the boy, picked him up and swung him high.

Sammy struggled to get down, and Jack let him. Then he sat and rubbed circles on his back.

Sammy went back to his bear, gently bouncing it.

"Up, down. Up, down." Arianna said the words in rhythm with the bear's bounces and watched Sammy for any recognition of the words.

"He doesn't talk," Jack said, his voice bleak. "I've done some reading, listened to some podcasts on autism. I guess that's part of it."

"It's probably a delay, right? Not a life sentence."

"I hope."

"When he heard your car, he sat there looking at the door until you came in. And when he wanted water instead of juice, he, um, *persisted* until I understood.

That's all communication." If Jack got discouraged, gave up on Sammy, she couldn't handle it.

"Thanks, Arianna." He gave her a brief, haggard smile. "And thanks for staying with him on no notice. It was kind of you." He gave the messy room another glance.

Oh brother. "Let me go clean up the kitchen," she said. "You stay here with Sammy."

"No, it's fine." Jack stood and followed her. "He plays well by himself."

She hurried in and knelt by the overturned trash can, stuffing garbage back into the container. When she looked up, Jack had stopped at the doorway, looking stunned.

"I'll clean it up!" She grabbed paper towels to wipe up the floor where the garbage had spilled, then rinsed her hands and started putting away beverage containers.

"Arianna." His hand on her shoulder felt big and warm and gentle. She sucked in a breath and went still.

He pulled his hand away. "It's okay. I can do this."

"No." She spun back toward the cracker-scattered counter to hide her discomfort, started brushing crackers and crumbs into the sink. "I made the mess. It's only fair I clean it up. See, especially for kids with disabilities, low blood sugar is the enemy. But you have all these special requirements—" she gestured toward the laminated sheets "—so it took a little longer."

"There's leftover chicken and rice in the fridge. You could have served him that."

"I didn't see it." But another, more practical person—like Chloe—would have looked harder.

"Look," he said, "I appreciate what you've done, more than you know. But right now, I'll be fine."

You didn't have to be a genius to read the subtext. *I want to be alone with my son.*

"Of course." She sidled past him out to the living room and found her purse. She knelt down by Sammy, swallowing hard. "Good to hang with you, little man," she whispered.

Then she went to the door, where Jack stood, no doubt impatient for her to go. "See ya," she said, aiming for breezy.

He tilted his head to one side. "You okay?"

She nodded quickly, forced a smile.

"Thanks again. Stay in touch."

Stay in touch. The same thing you'd say to a friend you encountered after some time away, a friend you really didn't much want to see again.

Her throat tightened, and she coughed harshly as she hurried to her car. She didn't deserve to cry.

Didn't deserve a job. Didn't deserve to spend time with Sammy. Didn't deserve any kind of warmth from her former brother-in-law, Jack.

She drove carefully down to the ranch's entrance, glanced back to make sure she was out of sight of Jack's new house, and then pulled off the road.

She drew deep breaths, trying to get calm, but it was impossible.

She'd just spent time—botched her time, really—with precious Sammy.

Her adopted nephew.

And, unknown to anyone on this earth but her and Sammy's adoption agency, her own biological son.

Chapter Two

The next Thursday, Jack walked out onto his porch with nanny candidate number four, Sammy in his arms. His son's wails died to a hiccup.

"Aw, he's such a cute peanut," the nineteen-year-old said, flicking a long lime-green fingernail under Sammy's chin, which made him cry again. "Just give me a call about when to start, okay?"

"Um, Mandy," Jack said to her retreating back. "I don't think this is going to work out."

She turned back in the process of extracting a cigarette from her purse. "What do you mean?"

"Sammy didn't seem to connect with you," he said. In the course of four nanny interviews, he'd learned to be blunt.

The teenager gave him a disbelieving stare. "He's *autistic*," she said, enunciating the word as if Jack were hard of hearing. "He's not *gonna* connect with people."

"Thanks for your time," he said, "but I won't be hiring you."

She lit her cigarette, inhaled deeply and blew out a

lungful of smoke. "What a waste coming up here. I *told* my mom I didn't like babysitting."

Jack blew out a breath as he watched her drive off and then sank down into one of the rockers on the porch, Sammy in his lap. "We dodged a bullet," he informed his son.

Sammy looked at him solemnly but made no answering sounds, and worry bloomed anew in Jack's chest. They needed to get started with treatment, but how could he find the time to interview nannies *and* therapeutic support staffers? He'd already maxed out Mrs. Jennings, his main caregiver in Esperanza Springs; although she'd assured him before that she'd be glad to continue babysitting Sammy after he moved, she'd quickly discovered she didn't like driving ten miles on mountain roads to get here. And Penny had been sweet, taking care of Sammy twice, but he couldn't continue asking that of the owner of Redemption Ranch.

From the newly renovated activities center, the sound of laughter made him turn his head. Four men emerged, one of them Carson Blair, his pastor, and another a veteran Jack knew a little. The other two were new to the ranch.

At their center was Arianna.

Before he knew it, he was on his feet, walking over.

"Everything okay here?" he asked. When the conversation abruptly died, he realized he must have sounded harsh.

Carson lifted an eyebrow. "We're fine over here, Jack. Something up with you?"

I don't like seeing Arianna surrounded by men, and I don't know why. "No, everything's fine," he said.

Arianna seemed oblivious to any undercurrents. "Oh,

hey," she said to Jack. "What's up with the little man?" She held out her arms for Sammy, and Jack was about to tell her not to bother, Sammy was upset. But his son considered her offer and then lifted his arms for her to pluck him from his father's hold.

Immediately, Sammy quieted down. Arianna nuzzled her cheek against his, looking blissful.

Gabe Smith, the veteran Jack had met a few times, greeted him with a friendly handshake. "Hey, Doc, I hate to ask it of you, but could you take a look at Rufus?" He gestured to the porch of the activities center, where a large gray-muzzled dog sprawled. "He's got a raw spot on his leg."

"Sure. I'll get my bag." *And pull myself together.*

He had no right to care what his sister-in-law—former sister-in-law—was up to. He had to focus on getting help for Sammy. Another nanny candidate was arriving soon, hopefully better than the last.

He brought out his bag, glanced over to make sure Sammy was still content with Arianna, and then joined Gabe on the porch. Examining Rufus would ground him. Dogs were so straightforward compared to people, and Rufus was a steady, respectable senior dog.

"Where's Bruiser?" he asked, and as if in answer, an elderly Chihuahua rushed out onto the porch, yipping. He postured stiff-legged in front of Rufus, teeth bared, growling at Jack.

"Hey, whoa, little buddy. I'm not gonna hurt your friend." He moved closer, sideways, not making eye contact, so as not to threaten the pint-size protector.

"Bruiser!" Gabe scolded. "Quit that." He picked up the little dog and sat down on the porch step, holding him.

Jack examined the hot spot Gabe was worried about

and bandaged it. "We don't want it to get infected. If he can just go a couple of days without licking it, it'll heal."

"Does he *have* to wear a collar of shame?" Gabe asked. "He hates it."

"I might have one of the new soft kind in the truck. It'll be more comfortable for him." He rubbed Rufus's big head and ears, and the dog lolled onto his back, panting.

Jack massaged the dog, enjoying the cool mountain breeze on his face. Despite his problems, he had a good life. New friends like Gabe, old friends like Penny, a healthy son, work he loved. And an environment where God's grandeur was continually on display.

When Arianna approached, Sammy in her arms, he was surprised to see the warm expression on her face.

He gave her a smile in return, and their eyes linked and stayed for a second longer than was polite. Heat washed over him.

A black PT Cruiser chugged up the road then, breaking the mood. It stopped in front of his place, and a woman stepped out. She looked to be a few years older than Jack and was dressed in black slacks and an old-fashioned white blouse. Her hair was caught back in a tight bun. She marched up to his front door and knocked.

"Uh-oh," he said. "Looks like Sammy and I have an appointment. Gabe, I'll dig out one of those collars for Rufus and bring it over later. You going to be home?" He waved a hand toward Gabe's cabin a short distance down the ranch's main road.

"Sure thing, we'll be around all day."

The nanny pounded on his door again and then returned to her car with visible exasperation. She got in and leaned on the horn.

A drop of rain fell, then another. The clouds that had been coming in clustered over them.

The prospective nanny got out of her car, snapped open a black umbrella and marched toward the cabin's porch again.

"You said you wanted Mary Poppins," Arianna murmured, a smile tugging at her mouth.

"So I did," he said with a sigh.

None of this was going to be as easy as he'd hoped.

"Thanks for letting me stay with you, Aunt Justine," Arianna said the next morning as she dodged stacks of magazines and newspapers to get their breakfast dishes to the kitchen sink.

"You're as welcome as can be," her aunt said. "I just wish the place were in better shape for visitors." She looked toward the hallway that led back to the bedrooms. "He won't let me throw anything away, and his stuff is filling up the whole house."

"I know how hard you try." Arianna submerged the dishes in soapy water and started to scrub. "I'm either going to find a job and a place to stay within the week, or I'll have to move back to Chicago."

"Don't do that!" Aunt Justine sounded horrified. "You should have settled down here like your sister did, not in that soulless city, when your parents moved overseas. I never could figure out why you chose to live there. I thought you loved it here, especially when you spent that one whole summer here during college."

Arianna rinsed the dishes and dunked a couple of dirty pans from the counter into the soapy water. It was good that Aunt Justine had never figured out the reason for Arianna's abrupt departure. Almost no one had known about the mistakes that had led to a surprise pregnancy. That was what had allowed Chloe to adopt Arianna's baby with no one the wiser.

Including Jack. Arianna sighed. She'd been adamantly opposed to Chloe keeping the truth from her husband. But Chloe had been as embarrassed about her infertility as Arianna was about her out-of-wedlock pregnancy. Somehow, adopting her sister's baby, and having people know it, made everything worse for Chloe.

And given how sensitive Chloe was, Arianna had given in. It was what she'd been raised to do. *Take care of your sister. She's not strong like you. Don't upset her.*

She pushed thoughts of her younger days out of her mind and asked Aunt Justine about her vegetable garden and the cat that had shown up on the doorstep yesterday. They had a nice chat while Arianna finished the washing up.

"There. That's better, at least." Arianna surveyed the empty sink and two feet of clear counter space with satisfaction. "Now, I'm going to go out and sell myself as an art therapist."

"Thank you for cleaning up, hon. I'll keep praying for a wonderful job for you."

Arianna strolled through the town of Esperanza Springs, inhaling the fresh scents of pine and sage that blew down from the Sangre de Cristo Mountains, watching a black-and-white magpie land on someone's fence post to scold the pedestrians walking by. From the Mountain High Bakery, the cinnamon scent was so powerful that Arianna was sorely tempted to pop in for a scone, even though she'd just had breakfast. But she didn't need to outgrow her summer clothes, so she walked resolutely past the bakery. She waved at the woman washing the windows of La Boca Feliz Mexican restaurant, and peeked in the hardware store window, then focused on her destination: the children's summer program housed in a local church. She was hoping they'd jump at the chance to have a real art therapist visit with the kids each week for the rest of the summer.

It had been a long shot, and she'd known it, but she was still disappointed at the firm no she got. Disappointed enough that she stopped in the town park to look out at the mountains, breathe in the fresh air and regroup.

She hadn't expected to land in a bed of roses when she'd come back to Esperanza Springs. She'd known the market for art therapists would be tiny; this town was about the basics, not the luxuries, and art therapy was considered a luxury by most of the folks around here.

The exception was up at Redemption Ranch. Penny and her staff were forward thinking; they knew that it took various types of therapy to reach veterans, to help them work through PTSD and other mental health issues related to their wartime service.

Maybe she could talk Penny into giving her more work than just the single class per week that she'd offered. And maybe one of the cabins was empty. If she could live rent-free...

It was another long shot, but at least it was worth trying. For the chance to live near her son, it was definitely worth a try. None of her attempts to put the past behind her and get on with her life had worked, so she hoped being near Sammy would help to settle her soul. That was the real reason she'd come back to Colorado.

Although, if Jack found out the truth, he'd be furious.

Understandably so. She and Chloe should never have kept something so important from him.

What if he got angry enough to keep her away from Sammy? Could he do that? Would he?

And what about Sammy, when he got old enough to wonder about his adoption and his birth parents?

She shook her head to try to shake off the circling thoughts and tuned back in to the world around her.

"That poor little thing," a woman was saying. She was on a bench behind Arianna, facing the playground. "They have no idea where he came from."

Idly, Arianna turned to see who the ladies were talking about.

And then she sucked in a breath. There was Sammy on the playground, just a few feet away from the women, toddling from the slide to the climbing structure, where a set of chimes was available for the kids to bang on.

"Turns out he has autism," the same woman said to a younger mom seated beside her, who was nursing a baby. "And now that I think about it, look how he just stands there banging on one thing over and over. I should have guessed."

"What's Dr. Jack gonna do? He's a widower, right?"

"I don't know, but I'm not as young as I used to be. And I didn't bargain for babysitting an autistic kid."

Arianna didn't know how she got to Sammy, but she found herself beside him, facing the two women on the bench. "Look," she said to the white-haired one, who'd been talking, "he's a child first. And he might not like to have his condition broadcast to everyone in the park."

"Who are *you*?" the white-haired woman asked.

That made Arianna pause, because she couldn't tell the whole truth, obviously. "I'm his aunt."

The woman pursed her lips. "I wasn't expecting to be eavesdropped on and criticized when I took this job," she said. "I've been planning to tell Dr. Jack I'm through. Maybe I'll just do it today. I don't need this."

Arianna studied her and saw tears behind the angry expression. "Look, maybe I spoke too harshly. I just feel like a child's medical condition is private."

"No, you're right, I'm a terrible babysitter." She sighed and held out a hand toward Sammy, who looked at her and then turned back to the chimes. "I talk too much, don't I, sugar? And you don't talk at all."

The other woman finished nursing her baby, packed up and hurried away with her little one.

"I shouldn't have said anything, maybe," Arianna said to Sammy's babysitter. "I just… Well, I was thinking, it's not other people's business what condition little Sammy has. Strangers, I mean. Like her." She gestured toward the rapidly departing young mother.

"I suppose," the woman said. "But honestly, I have to talk to someone. I can't deal with all the things this child is going to need. Dr. Jack is lovely, but he brought up supervising therapists and having people come to the home to work with him each day… I didn't sign up for that. I'm retired. We didn't even *have* autism when I was growing up."

Well, they'd had it, they just hadn't diagnosed it, but whatever. "I'm sure it can all be worked out. Jack and Sammy really need the help."

"I'm overwhelmed," the woman admitted. "I'm also a grandma, and I'm not sure whether my grandkids should be around him. Oh, not that he'll hurt them or anything, but they might be too rough or tease him. It's just all so complicated."

"I'm sure Jack will help," she said soothingly, watching Sammy. Did he really act autistic? Was he banging for an unusually long time on those chimes?

Maybe he was exhibiting musical talent. How could you even tell the difference?

Just then Sammy saw them watching and toddled over, arms extended toward Arianna.

"See, and he never comes to me. And he doesn't speak. He's a difficult child to work with."

Arianna picked Sammy up and held him loosely against her. "Do you have one of his toys?"

The woman fumbled through her bag, but she was obviously more intent on venting her feelings as she absentmindedly handed Arianna a cloth block that jingled when shaken. "I don't think he likes me," she said.

"He might just not be very expressive," Arianna said, feeling defensive for Sammy. "Kids with autism don't always smile a lot." How had this turned into a coaching session for a woman more than twice her age?

And what if the coaching didn't work and the woman decided to quit?

"To think, I'm sitting here in the park and getting in trouble for a chat I have with an acquaintance." The woman waved off in the direction of the woman who'd left with her baby. "You know what? I've had enough. You're his aunt, you say?"

Arianna nodded. She was getting a very bad feeling.

"He obviously knows and likes you. Better than he likes me." The woman stood and plunked the diaper bag into Arianna's lap. "Here," she said. "You take care of him. His father will be here in half an hour. Tell him he can mail me my last paycheck."

"But…but…"

It was no use. The woman left, and there was Arianna, literally left holding the bag.

The bag, and her secret son.

Chapter Three

Jack's last Saturday appointment was with a longtime patient: Mr. McCrady's Irish setter, Cider. He ran his fingers over the dog's hunched haunches and manipulated her legs, noticing when the stoic creature gave a little flinch. "Her arthritis is bothering her more?"

"Hers and mine, both." Mr. McCrady's forehead wrinkled as he stroked his dog's ears. "She has trouble getting out of her bed some mornings. Can we get her on pain meds?"

"Absolutely." Jack finished the exam and then scratched Cider's chest, glad to note that her plume of a tail wagged. "There are risks to her kidneys that come with that type of medication, so we'll want to keep up with her bloodwork. But I think she's earned some pain relief."

"That she has," Mr. McCrady said. "She's been my best friend since my wife died. I don't know what I'd do without her."

The dog panted, seeming to smile up at her owner. Her white face and warm brown eyes communicated pure, uncomplicated love. Jack had really come to appreciate senior dogs since he'd been working at Redemption Ranch.

He got Mr. McCrady and Cider set with a prescription and an appointment for a follow-up visit and then stepped into his office to check messages.

He skimmed past seven he could handle later, and then his fingers froze.

Why was Arianna messaging him?

Problem with your sitter. I have Sammy and he's fine. Come to my aunt's house, 30 Maple Ave. ASAP

A problem with his sitter? He scrolled on through but didn't see a message from Mrs. Jennings.

"Gotta run," he said to his receptionist, who was gathering up her things. "There's an issue with Sammy. Can you and Thomas close up?"

"Sure thing, Doc. Hope everything's okay."

Jack drove the four blocks to Maple Avenue without his usual pauses to enjoy the town's Saturday bustle and then hurried up the front sidewalk to Arianna's aunt's house. He'd been here a couple of times in the early days of his marriage, but Chloe hadn't gotten along with her aunt and uncle—hadn't gotten along with a lot of people, including Arianna—so he didn't know them well.

When he rang the doorbell, Arianna's aunt Justine answered. "Hey, Dr. Jack, you sure you want to come into the craziness?"

"I got a message that my son's here," he said.

"In the kitchen." She gestured behind her. "Come on in."

Jack's eyes widened at the stacks of magazines and

newspapers that allowed only a narrow path through the hallway.

"I don't want any more people in here!" came a bellow from the other end of the house.

"It's just Dr. Jack," Aunt Justine yelled back. "He's here to get his baby."

"Well, send him on his way."

She gave Jack an apologetic shrug. "Go on in and see Arianna and Sammy. He—" she gestured in the direction from which her husband's shout had come "—he's embarrassed about how the house looks. I just have to calm him down." Justine turned and hurried toward the back of the house.

Jack picked his way through the mess, his uneasiness growing.

When he got to the kitchen, his focus immediately went to Sammy. His son sat straight-legged on a clean blanket next to Arianna, who was talking at a computer screen.

Sammy held a wooden spoon and was tapping it against a plastic bowl with intense concentration.

"I have experience with teenagers, yes," Arianna was saying to the screen. Her wild curls were pulled back into a neat bun, and her peach-colored shirt was more tailored and buttoned-up than what she usually wore.

She also had a streak of what looked like blueberry jam across her cheek that matched the streaks on Sammy's shirt. Oops.

"I'm staying with relatives in Esperanza Springs right now," she said, apparently in answer to an interview question. "But I'm able to relocate for the right job."

She was doing a Skype interview and, for whatever reason, she was also taking care of his son.

And she was thinking about relocating? Jack's chest tightened.

But he didn't have time to wonder what *that* was about. "Come here, buddy," he said quietly, holding out his hands to pick up Sammy. The steady banging noise his son was making couldn't help Arianna's cause.

Sammy noticed him for the first time and pumped his little arms. Jack's heart lifted, and he swung Sammy up.

But not before Sammy's flailing feet made a stack of plastic containers clatter to the ground. The noise startled Sammy, and he began to cry.

Jack glanced at Arianna in time to see her slight cringe. The person doing the interview, blurry on the screen, frowned.

"I can send you reference letters or give you phone numbers," Arianna said over the din.

She turned up the sound and Jack heard the fatal words: "We'll be in touch."

He carried Sammy out of the room, waved to Justine, who stood at the end of a hallway arguing with her husband, and went out the front door. He started toward his truck, then paused. He needed to get Sammy home, but first, he'd better wait and find out from Arianna what was going on. And apologize for disrupting her job interview.

Putting Sammy down on his blanket, he showed him a smooth stick. True to form, Sammy found it fascinating and began to bang it on the ground.

It wasn't three minutes before Arianna came out. "Hey," she said when she saw him.

"How'd your job interview go?" he asked. "I'm sorry for all the noise."

She shrugged. "What will be will be," she said. "I

was just hoping... It's my only semilocal opportunity."
Her words were casual, but her eyes were upset. She was
fingering her necklace, and Jack saw that it was a cross.

Yeah, he'd heard she'd come to the faith in a big way.

"So what happened with Sammy?"

She sighed. "It's my fault."

"What's your fault?" Arianna meant well, but chaos
followed her wherever she went. Chloe had always said
as much.

"The sitter was talking about his autism in the park,
where everyone could hear," she said. "I sort of got upset
and told her she shouldn't share his diagnosis—which
wasn't my business, and I'm sorry—and she ended up
dumping him and all his stuff on me."

"She was talking about his diagnosis? At the park?"

"She didn't mean any harm. I think she was just trying to figure out how to cope."

That sounded like Mrs. Jennings.

Sammy looked up, and Jack sat down to be closer,
rubbing his son's back. How was he going to do right
by Sammy? The child needed careful, consistent care,
and he'd known for a while that Mrs. Jennings couldn't
fit the bill, even before they'd gotten the diagnosis. But
now, his interviews with so-called serious sitters weren't
going any better. He'd even tried Skyping with a couple
of women from out of state, but he'd not gotten a warm
feeling from any of them.

"I don't know what I'm going to do," he said. Right
now, he felt like just a struggling dad and was glad to
have a relative to vent to, someone who seemed to care
about Sammy almost as much as he did.

She tilted her head to one side. "This could be a God
thing."

"What do you mean?"

"I need a job," she said slowly. "And you need a nanny."

He saw where she was going and let his eyes close. "Look, Arianna, I don't want to hurt your feelings. But I just don't think—"

"*Don't* think, then," she said.

"But I'm responsible for—"

"Don't think—pray." She stood smoothly, leaned down and ran a finger across Sammy's shoulders—which he normally hated, but accepted from Arianna with just an upward glance—and then walked toward her car.

"Arianna…"

"Don't answer now. Pray about it," she called over her shoulder. "See you at church tomorrow."

The next morning, Arianna thought about how much she loved art. One reason was the way it distracted you from your problems. It had distracted little Suzy Li from missing her mom, right here in the second-grade Sunday school class, and it had distracted Arianna from thinking about her own ridiculous offer to Jack DeMoise the day before.

"I'm sorry Suzy got a little paint on her shirt," she said to Mrs. Li as Suzy tugged her mom's hand, pulling her over to look at the picture she'd painted, now drying on a clothesline with the rest of the primary kids' paintings.

"I'm just thrilled she made it through the whole class," Mrs. Li said in between hugging Suzy and admiring her picture. "It's been a long time since I've gotten to stay for a whole church service. What a big girl you were, Suzy!"

"I missed you, Mommy." Suzy wrapped her arms around her mother. "But Miss Arianna said I was brave."

Mrs. Li smiled at Arianna. *Thank you*, she mouthed.

Arianna was glad she'd helped, but she felt a pang; she couldn't deny it. It was fun and rewarding to get her kid fix through helping with Sunday school, but in the end, those precious little ones wanted their own mommies. In the end, Arianna went home alone.

Fortunately, there was no time to dwell on what she didn't have. Sunny and Skye, the pastor's twins, needed their hands washed before heading out with their mom, who introduced herself as Lily. "Don't worry about it," Lily said as Arianna tried to scrub off the paint that had inexplicably splattered both twins' arms. "As long as they're happy, it's fine."

"That's what I said." Kayla, the main teacher of the primary-age kids and the mother of one of them, Leo, came over, and she and Lily hugged. "Kids are supposed to get messy and have fun."

Yeah, they were right about kids, Arianna thought, but what about her? When was she going to grow up and stop getting messy? She wet a paper towel and used it to wipe the biggest smudge from her cheek. The green streak in her hair was probably there to stay, at least until she could get back to her temporary home and shower.

"Hey, Dr. D," Kayla said and went to the door to greet Jack, who was leaning in with Sammy parked on his hip. Arianna sucked in a breath. He was good-looking to begin with, but when he smiled, he was breathtaking.

Finn Gallagher, Kayla's husband, showed up and sidled past Jack into the classroom. He reached out to Kayla and gently rubbed her shoulders, his eyes crinkling. She smiled up at him, love and happiness written all over her face.

Arianna's chest tugged. What would it be like to have someone touch you as if you were infinitely precious? Someone with whom to share your deepest thoughts, your hopes and dreams, your secrets?

But she couldn't tell anyone her deepest secrets, not and have them look at her the way Finn looked at Kayla. An out-of-wedlock pregnancy wasn't that uncommon, and there were plenty of people who took it in stride, raised the child and got on with their lives. Arianna wished she was that person, but she wasn't. Not given her family and the way she was raised.

As a result, she'd given away her child…and lied about it.

Jack was still standing at the half door. "Are you coming to the church lunch?" he asked her abruptly.

She hesitated. The church had a lunch after services every Sunday, for members and anyone in the community who needed a free meal or fellowship. She should go, since she was trying to make some kind of a life here. "Um, I guess."

"Good. I'll see you there." And he was off.

What did *that* mean? That he wanted to see her, have lunch with her, hang out, accept her offer of helping with Sammy? Or that he wanted to let her down easy?

She blew out a sigh as she wiped down the tables where the kids had been painting. Thanks to an abundance of newspapers, cleanup wasn't that difficult, but she found herself lingering, carefully putting things away in a most uncharacteristic way.

She knew why she was stalling: she didn't want to go

to the lunch and face Jack. Not after she'd made such a ridiculous offer.

Why had she suggested—again—that she could serve as Sammy's nanny when Jack clearly didn't want her to? Had she turned into one of those desperate women who couldn't take no for an answer?

Jack was kind and he would be nice about it, but rejection was rejection. She wasn't looking forward to it.

But, oh, for the chance to take care of her son, even briefly! To get to know him, to help him, to watch him grow.

No, said the stern voice in her head. She didn't deserve it, and it wasn't for her.

She was tempted to just skip the lunch and go home, avoiding Jack altogether, except she didn't have a home, not really. Aunt Justine and Uncle Steve had been kind to take her in, and hospitable, but trying to make space for another person in their crowded home was putting a strain on their relationship. She could see it. The more hours she could stay away the better.

Which pointed to her other problem: she needed to make new living arrangements. It was just that she didn't know whether to make them here or somewhere else.

Meanwhile, she'd get her aunt and uncle take-out meals from the church lunch, she decided. It was so hard to cook anything in their kitchen, piled high with appliance boxes and recycling and newspapers. It wasn't much, but a good meal from the church would be a small token of her gratitude to them.

Penny caught up with her and walked alongside. "You doing okay? You look a little blue."

She couldn't tell Penny the big reason, of course. "Just thinking about my living situation," she said as they walked into the fellowship hall, where the meal was already being served. "I'm wearing out my welcome at my aunt and uncle's place, but I'm on a tight budget until I find more work."

"Hmm, that's tough." And then Penny snapped her fingers and stared at her. "You know what? The pastor was right. With God all things are possible."

"Oh, I know that's true—"

Penny interrupted her. "No, seriously. I just got a brainstorm."

"What's that?"

"I've got a mother-in-law apartment upstairs at my house on the ranch, and I've been meaning to clean it out and fix it up forever. You're energetic and artsy. How would you like to stay there for the next few weeks? Rent-free, if you'll clean it and fix it up nice, so I can rent it out at the end of the summer."

Arianna's jaw dropped. "That would be so perfect!"

And then the other ramifications of Penny's offer rushed into her mind.

She could live so close to Sammy. Across the lawn, basically.

But how would Jack feel about that? Would she appear to be stalking him?

Penny was studying her face and no doubt saw her mixed feelings. "You think about it," she said. "There's no need to decide today."

"Thank you." Arianna gripped Penny's hand, her eyes filling with tears. "That's such a kind, kind offer. I just… have to figure a few things out, but I'm incredibly grateful to you for suggesting it."

"I'd be getting as much out of it as you are," Penny

said. "Now, you'd better go grab a bite to eat while they're still serving."

Arianna did just that, accepting a generous portion of enchiladas, rice and beans. She sat down next to an older woman who introduced herself as Florence, and they chatted a little while Arianna ate.

The fellowship hall was just a big tile-floored room with a stage at one end and a kitchen at the other. Long tables covered with cheerful red-checked tablecloths and lined by metal folding chairs filled one half of the room. Only about half the seats were full now; Arianna had lingered in the kids' room long enough that people were finishing up and heading home.

All of a sudden, Florence's eyes sharpened. "Would you look at that," she said, nodding toward a woman who was settling her two children at the other end of the table. "Pregnant with kid number three and not a husband in sight."

Arianna registered the disapproval and was aware that she would have faced the same if she'd kept Sammy. But she couldn't tear her eyes away from the woman, smiling and tickling her toddler while a slightly older child clung to her leg.

It would have been so wonderful to keep Sammy. And while she knew there had been many blessings in his adoption placement—not least his responsible, loving father, who was seated with Sammy at the far end of the room, where it was quieter—she couldn't help but wish she'd found a way to keep her baby, to raise him herself.

Then she wouldn't be caught in this web of lies, trying to decide whether it would be possible to live next door to her son without revealing her true relationship to him.

She barely realized she was staring dreamily into

space until Florence waved a hand in front of her face. "I think Dr. Jack is trying to get your attention," she said, her eyes alight with curiosity. "You'd better go talk to him."

Arianna snapped to awareness, looked in Jack's direction and saw that he was indeed beckoning to her.

Quickly, she finished her last bites of rice and beans. "It was nice talking to you," she said to her extremely observant neighbor. She took both their dishes to the washing area and then headed over to Jack, mixed gladness and dread in her heart.

Any day she could see Sammy was a good day. But she was pretty sure Jack was about to turn down her nanny offer. And then she'd have to tell Penny she couldn't take the apartment, and leave.

The thought of being away from her son after spending precious time with him made her chest ache, and she blinked away unexpected tears as she approached Jack and Sammy.

Sammy didn't look up at her. He was holding up one finger near his own face, moving it back and forth.

Jack caught his hand. "Say hi, Sammy! Here's Aunt Arianna."

Sammy tugged his hands away and continued to move his finger in front of his face.

"Sammy, come on."

Sammy turned slightly away from his father and refocused on his fingers.

"It's okay," Arianna said, because she could see the beginnings of a meltdown. "He doesn't need to greet me. What's up?"

"Look," he said, "I've been thinking about what you

said." He rubbed a hand over the back of his neck, clearly uncomfortable.

Sammy's hands moved faster, and he started humming a wordless tune. It was almost as if he could sense the tension between Arianna and Jack.

"It's okay, Jack," she said. "I get it. My being your nanny was a crazy idea." Crazy, but oh, so appealing. She ached to pick Sammy up and hold him, to know that she could spend more time with him, help him learn, get him support for his special needs.

But it wasn't her right.

"Actually," he said, "that's what I wanted to talk about. It does seem sort of crazy, but…I think I'd like to offer you the job."

She stared at him, her eyes filling. "Oh, Jack," she said, her voice coming out in a whisper. Had he really just said she could have the job?

Behind her, the rumble and snap of tables being folded and chairs being stacked, the cheerful conversation of parishioners and community people, faded to an indistinguishable murmur.

She was going to be able to be with her son. Every day. She reached out and stroked Sammy's soft hair, and even though he ignored her touch, her heart nearly melted with the joy of being close to him.

Jack's brow wrinkled. "On a trial basis," he said. "Just for the rest of the summer, say."

Of course. She pulled her hand away from Sammy and drew in a deep breath. She needed to calm down and take things one step at a time. Yes, leaving him at the end of the summer would break her heart ten times more. But even a few weeks with her son was more time than she deserved.

"Would you like to go get a cup of coffee?" he asked. "Nail down the details? I think Penny would be willing to take Sammy for an hour or two."

Arianna found her voice. "That's okay," she said, trying not to sound as breathless as she felt. "We can just talk it over at your house. Or here. Wherever."

He frowned and cleared his throat. "I'd like to be a little more formal and organized about it," he said as he started to collect Sammy's things into his utilitarian gray diaper bag. "Draw up a contract, that sort of thing. We need to hammer out the terms."

Hammer out the terms. What were the right terms for an aunt to become nanny to her secret son? "Okay, sure, I guess."

"Meet you at the coffee shop in half an hour?"

"Sure." Dazed, she turned and headed out to her car.

With God all things are possible. The pastor had said it, and she'd just witnessed its truth. She was being given a job, taking care of her son and had a place to live.

It was a blessing, a huge one. But it came at a cost: she was going to need to conceal the truth from Jack on a daily basis. And given the way her heart was jumping around in her chest, she wondered if she was going to be able to survive this much of God's blessing.

Chapter Four

Jack walked into the coffee shop half an hour later, still in his business-casual church clothes, briefcase in hand. He had a sample contract on a clipboard, a tablet to take notes, his calendar on his phone.

Having all his supplies made him feel slightly more in charge of a situation that seemed to be spiraling out of control.

He felt uneasy and uncomfortable and wrong every time he thought about hiring Arianna as a nanny, even temporarily. Partly, it was what he knew about her being disorganized and messy. More than that was the fact that Chloe had had real issues with her sister and would never have approved of her taking care of Sammy.

And even more than all that, he just felt strangely uncomfortable with his former sister-in-law.

When he thought about Sammy, though, he knew what he had to do, what was right. Sammy liked Arianna, and she was good with him. And they needed to start his treatment now, not when the perfect nanny showed up in six months or a year.

Inside the shop, the deep, rich fragrance of good

coffee soothed him. He waved to a few patrons and headed for the counter. He'd order before Arianna got here, get her some coffee, too.

"Jack!" came a sunny voice from the other side of the shop.

He looked up and saw a mass of coppery curls, then Arianna's wide smile. His muscles tightened, and he felt a strong urge to back out the door. Stronger was the urge to go toward her, even though it felt like he just might be headed for disaster.

She gestured him over, holding up a drink. "I already got you something!" she called over the buzz of the small crowd.

As Jack turned and walked toward her, he was aware of several people watching. Arianna wasn't quiet.

And she'd gotten him one of those expensive whipped-cream-topped iced coffee drinks he didn't even like.

"Thanks," he said as he reached the table and sat down. "You didn't have to do that. How much was it?" He got out his wallet.

"It's on me," she said. "You've got to try this. I had one the other day and it's so good! It's a mocha java supreme. Of course, I shouldn't have it, it's full of calories, but you certainly don't need to worry about calories."

"Thanks." He sat down, feeling concerned, and studied her. She was talking fast, even for Arianna. She was stressed out, too, he realized, as much as or more than he was.

Compassion washed over him then. Arianna was living in that hoarder house with her aunt and uncle and probably very low on cash. She needed this job, and his own worries paled.

He got out his clipboard and notes. "Before we start

going through this," he said, "are you sure you're interested in the job? It'll be more responsibility than most
nanny jobs, because you'd be supervising some of his
therapists and doing the exercises they suggest. You'd
have days off, of course, but you wouldn't be able to
pursue a full-time art therapy position."

"I'm sure," she said, her eyes shining.

He got tangled up in that gaze for a few seconds, then
looked away and cleared his throat. "Okay, then. Most
of the sample contracts I looked at—" he pulled out the
one he'd printed to show her "—have clauses about what
will happen if either party decides to back out early. And
we need to nail down an equitable schedule so you don't
get burned-out." He drew a breath to continue.

She put a hand over his. "Jack. I trust you. Whatever
you think is best."

Her hand on his felt soft and delicate and warm.

He straightened and pulled his hand away. "I can draft
a schedule if that would work for you. Then we can go
over it and finalize the details. Now, let's talk about pay."

"I'd do it for free," she said promptly.

"Arianna!" Jack shook his head, frowning at her.
"You should never say that to a potential employer."

"You're not just that, you're my former brother-in-law.
And Sammy is my nephew. Jack, we don't have to hash
out every single detail, nor get everything down in writing. We can make it happen with a handshake."

He pointed his mechanical pencil at her. "You're way
too trusting. People will take advantage of you."

To his surprise, she nodded. "It's happened before,"
she said. "But should I let that change me into a suspicious person?"

He really wanted to know who'd taken advantage of

her, because he wanted to strangle that person. Some guy, most likely. "Not a suspicious person," he said, "but maybe a cautious one."

"You're probably right," she said with a shrug. "But for now...I'm super excited to be working with Sammy. I know I can help him."

Jack had to admit that her attitude was enormously appealing. If a stranger he was interviewing had acted so enthusiastically, he'd have hired her immediately. Well, after checking her résumé and background, of course. Unlike Arianna, he wasn't impulsive.

And there were a lot of details to straighten out. "Now, as far as where you'll stay," he said. "I have plenty of room in the house, but I'm afraid that would raise a few eyebrows. I wouldn't want your reputation to suffer."

"Or yours," she said, sipping her drink. "But actually, I've got it covered. Penny offered me the use of her upstairs apartment if I'll clean it out and decorate it so she can rent it in the fall."

"That's perfect." Another thing that was working out better than he expected. Not what he was used to. He often expected the worst.

He plowed on through his list of things to discuss. "How do you feel about organizing the TSS schedule? Is that something you can handle?"

A smile quirked the corner of her mouth. "I *can* be organized, Jack," she said with exaggerated patience. "I'm just not when it doesn't matter."

It's important to sweat the small stuff, he heard in his mind. Chloe's voice. The same as his mother's and father's. Chloe had gotten along so well with them, partly because she'd tried so hard to do everything right.

Guilt suffused him. Chloe hadn't trusted Arianna and

wouldn't think that hiring her was doing things right. She'd never sanction this arrangement.

Arianna fumbled in her oversize bag and brought out a tablet computer. "I can print this out for you later, if you want," she said. "It's my résumé." She enlarged it so he could see. "I've taken two classes focused on kids with special needs. They were a little older than Sammy, but the principles are the same." She scrolled to another section. "And I did an internship in an early-childhood program. I love babies." For just a moment, her eyes went wistful.

Jack studied those eyes as questions he'd never thought to ask before pressed into his awareness. Had Arianna wanted to have kids? Did she ever think about it? Was there a boyfriend in the picture?

Around them, the buzz of conversation indicated that the coffee shop was getting crowded. But Jack couldn't seem to look away from Arianna.

She didn't seem nearly so affected. "This section is my coursework," she continued on, scrolling down the tablet's screen and highlighting a section to show him. "We did a lot of psychology, life-span development, counseling work. Here, take a look." She handed him the tablet.

He scanned it quickly, then read more closely, impressed. "You have so much coursework in special education."

She laughed, a sunny, lilting sound. "Don't look so shocked, Jack. It's part of most art and music therapy programs."

He met her eyes over the tablet and couldn't avoid smiling, almost as big as she did. "There's a lot more to you than meets the eye, isn't there?"

"You haven't scratched the surface." Was there a tiny bit of flirtation in her tone, in her expression as she looked at him over the rim of her cup?

He took a long pull on his own drink, sucking up frothy sweetness. "You know," he said, "these are actually good."

Again, their gazes tangled.

"Son!" The deep voice penetrated his awareness at the same time a familiar, beefy hand gripped his shoulder.

He glanced up as the usual tension squeezed his chest. He knew *exactly* what his father was thinking. "Hi, Dad. Do you remember—"

"Arianna Shrader. How could I forget." His father didn't extend his hand for shaking and neither did she, instead inclining her head slightly, as if she were a queen and he, a lowly peasant.

The attitude wasn't lost on Dad, Jack could see. But looking at Arianna, he could tell his father's attitude wasn't lost on her, either.

"What brings about this meeting?" Disapproval dripped from his father's voice.

"I'm going to be working for Jack," Arianna said. "Taking care of Sammy for a while."

"You're *what*?" Dad's voice squeaked, and his face reddened. He looked at Jack as if he'd just committed a federal crime. "Was this *your* idea?"

"It was my idea," Arianna interjected before Jack could open his mouth. "It made sense, given my background and Jack's needs. Is there a problem?"

"Sure seems like a problem to me, you moving in with your sister's husband."

Arianna gasped.

At the same moment, Jack stood and stepped forward

so that he was in between his father and Arianna. "Arianna is Sammy's aunt," he said, "and there's nothing inappropriate about her caring for him."

"Perceptions mean a lot," Dad said, but his voice was quieter. He stepped sideways to look at Arianna. "It's your reputation that would suffer the most. This is a small town."

"I won't be living in." Arianna's normally expressive eyes were cool and flat. "Your son's virtue is safe with me."

His father's face went almost purple, his mouth opening and closing like a dying fish.

"It's under control, Dad." Jack put a hand on his father's arm. "Nothing to worry about."

Dad looked at their half-empty cups, pursed his lips and shook his head. "I hope so," he said abruptly and walked away, weaving through the coffee shop's small tables.

"I'm sorry for that," Jack said. "Dad can be a little…"

"Judgmental? I'm familiar," Arianna said, and suddenly, Jack wondered what kinds of things his father had said to her on the few occasions they'd all gotten together.

Certainly, the buoyancy had gone out of her face and voice, and he continued to think about that as they agreed on a few last details and a start date—tomorrow.

But as he walked her to her car, Jack couldn't forget what his father had said. Perceptions were important. At least a few people in their small town might start to link their names together.

Chloe would have felt that as the ultimate disrespect. If that wretched blood clot hadn't already killed her, this would have.

Was he making a huge mistake hiring Arianna?

* * *

"The place is kind of a mess," Penny warned Arianna that evening as they climbed the outside steps to Arianna's new apartment. "It's been a rough year."

Arianna had heard bits and pieces of Penny's story: how she and her husband had bought the ranch with high hopes. How they'd worked together—she with enthusiasm for the mission, he with enthusiasm for their pretty young office assistant. How he'd left Penny high and dry, and absconded with the funds *and* the assistant.

Penny was so kind and so beautiful, Arianna couldn't imagine how anyone could do that to her.

But then again, men could quickly tire of a woman when there were responsibilities involved, or when they found a new obsession. She'd learned that the hard way from Sammy's father.

Penny threw open the door at the top of the steps, then put a hand on Arianna's arm, stopping her. "You'd be doing me a favor if you'd move in and fix it up, but it'll be a lot of work. You be honest, now. If it's too much for you, say no. I'll understand."

Little did Penny realize how few options Arianna actually had. "I'm sure it'll be fine," she assured the older woman. "I love a good project." Not least because it would keep her busy and push her worries away.

"Just take a look before you say anything," Penny said and held the door for Arianna to walk through.

Inside, hard-back chairs stood at odd angles amid boxes, a big cooler and a bike that had to date from the 1980s. The place smelled musty, and through the giant dirty window, sunbeams illuminated the dust motes that danced in the air.

Arianna looked past the surface, something she'd always loved to do. The place had great bones and amazing potential. She clasped her hands together. "This is perfect!"

"You're kidding, right?"

"No! That slanted wood ceiling is gorgeous. I love a nonboxy space. And the view from the windows... It'll look out on mountains, right?"

"The Sangre de Cristos, once it's clean. You can barely see them through that coating of dirt and dust." Penny picked up a photo album covered in white lace. She grimaced at the happy couple on the cover and then dropped the album into the trash.

Arianna lifted an eyebrow but didn't comment. Not her business.

She looked around, scoping out the space. "I'd put the bed there," she said, gesturing to a space directly across from the big window. "Wall hangings should be big, with these tall ceilings. A sitting area over here." As she spoke, the place came to life in her imagination. "It's so much more than I expected in a place to live."

Penny put her hands on her hips and stared at her. "Now, why would you say that? Where were you living before, that this place seems so fabulous?"

Arianna flushed. "Oh, just here and there." No need to tell Penny about how unsettled the past couple of years had been, and how she hadn't been able to commit to anything since giving up her son. "Two days ago I was out of a job and practically out of a home, and now I have both." She bit her lip and shot up a prayer of thanks. "God's so good."

Even as she spoke, worry crept in. Penny was wise and saw a lot. Would she guess the truth about Sammy? Would Jack?

They worked together hauling boxes down the stairs

and throwing them into the ranch foreman's truck. "Finn said once it's full, he'll drive it over to the dump," Penny said.

"Just look at the floor," Arianna commented once a big square of it was cleared. "With a bright rug and a polish, these plank floors will come to life."

"You're so positive," Penny said. "You're going to be good for Jack." She hesitated, then added, "In a way your sister wasn't."

"Oh!" Color rose in Arianna's face. "It's not the same at all. I'm just the temporary nanny." Jack had made that very clear. He'd sent her a text after their conversation just to confirm that she understood that.

Penny didn't seem to have heard her. "His parents were so rigid. His mom's passed, rest her soul, but his dad seems to have gotten even more… What? Judgmental? Tense? Your sister had some of those same qualities." Penny smiled at her. "It strikes me that you don't."

Yes, true, to her detriment. She'd been the one to get pregnant without being married and disgrace the family. While poor Chloe, always such a perfectionist—and so perfect—hadn't been able to have the one thing that meant everything to her: a baby.

"Anyone home?" came a call from downstairs.

"We're up here, Willie." Penny brushed the back of her hand over her sweaty forehead and gestured toward a door Arianna hadn't seen before. "This is where the downstairs connects. You can lock the door for privacy or come down to use the laundry machines whenever you want."

A short, rotund but muscular man with a long gray ponytail huffed up the steps. "There you are," he said, sweeping off his Vietnam veterans hat. He gave Arianna a quick nod, but his eyes were fixed on Penny. "Can I offer you lovely ladies some help? Before I offer to take you to lunch?" he added to Penny.

Color rose in Penny's cheeks. "Willie, have you met Arianna? She's going to be living here and working as a nanny for Jack."

Willie smiled at her, his face breaking into a million creases. "I'm pleased to meet you," he said. "That Jack works hard. He could use some help." He turned back toward Penny. "Now, what about that lunch?"

Penny gestured at her dusty work clothes. "Look at me. I can't possibly go out. And we wouldn't ask you to do our grunt work."

"I was a grunt in the service," Willie said with a wink at Arianna. "The company's a lot better here."

"No, thanks, Willie," Penny said. "Another time."

"Maybe tomorrow night?" he asked. "I've got a gift card for the Cold Creek Inn. You could wear that red dress you have."

Penny's cheeks went pink. "I... We'll see," she said and turned back to the box she'd been sorting through.

"Talk her into it, will you?" he asked Arianna. "You know where to find me," he added to Penny and then descended the stairs.

"Looks like you have an admirer," Arianna said, waggling her eyebrows at Penny.

"Oh, he's just lonely because his friend Long John is off on his honeymoon," Penny said. "Those two have been best friends forever and lived next door in the ranch cabins until just recently. Long John married a woman from town, Beatrice Patton, just as soon as her chemo treatments ended. I think they kind of bonded over their health issues, since Long John has Parkinson's."

"Wow." The older woman's matter-of-fact words put Arianna's own problems into perspective.

"Anyway," Penny continued, "Long John getting married and moving down to town is an adjustment for Willie."

"I don't know if the invitation is all about missing his friend," Arianna teased. "I doubt he'd want Long John to wear a red dress to lunch."

"Oh, stop it!" Penny said, laughing a little. "Willie's a nice man, but…"

"He's older than you are. By kind of a lot."

"It's not that. It's that I'm not ready." Penny sighed. "Truth is, when my husband left me, he took that part of me that used to trust people. Or trust men anyway."

"I can understand that." Arianna hadn't dated anyone since Sammy's father for that very reason. But while her own loneliness felt well deserved, Penny's made her sad. "Sounds like he just wants to take you to dinner. Maybe you should go."

"I don't want him to spend his gift card on me. He'd think it means more than it does, and I don't want to hurt anyone, but especially someone who lives on the ranch. We have to be able to coexist."

Coexist. That was what she and Jack had to learn to do, too. But it was hard to look at it so impersonally when there was a child involved.

His child. Her child.

The sound of footsteps trotting up the steps interrupted their conversation. There was a tap on the door, and Jack's face appeared in the glass. "Need any help?" he asked.

Yes, Arianna wanted to say. *Can you help me make my heart stop pounding?*

"Absolutely," Penny said. "We have a bunch of boxes that need to be moved down to Finn's truck. You look like just the man for the job."

"It's good to be needed," Jack said. "Sammy's TSS kicked me out. She said I was hovering."

"Is Sammy okay being alone with her?" Arianna stood and looked out the window toward Jack's house.

"For now, yes," he said. "She has me on speed dial, and I'm to stay within shouting distance. She and Sammy were doing work with his vocalizing and I was distracting him, apparently."

"Do they know what caused his autism?" The question seemed to burst out of her. She hadn't even known she was wondering that. But she must've spoken intensely, because the other two stared at her.

"No one knows for sure," Jack said. "There's definitely a genetic component, and there's a lot about Sammy's background we don't know, given that it was a closed adoption. There's supposed to be a work-around if he develops any health problems, so maybe…" He trailed off.

Arianna's stomach roiled. She couldn't talk about Sammy's genetics with Jack. She couldn't hold it together, couldn't keep him from guessing the truth. At the same time, she wanted to do anything she could to help her son. "Would it make a difference if his genetics were known?" She tried hard to keep the question casual.

"I don't think so. We're still diving into the same type of intervention, and as early as possible. As you'll find out, the more you're around him and his therapists."

"I'm looking forward to working with him." And she should change the subject. She pointed toward the corner of the room. "Those boxes over there need carrying down."

Had she pulled it off? Or did both Penny and Jack think she was acting weird?

Fortunately, her worries were interrupted by another knock, this one on the downstairs door.

Penny rolled her eyes. "I can go weeks without anyone ever coming to visit, but today, when I'm trying to get something done, it's Grand Central Station." She headed down the stairs.

That left Arianna alone when Jack trotted back up the steps. "Ready for another load," he said.

Arianna indicated a stack of three boxes. "You take two. I'll take one," she said, trying for a businesslike tone.

But as she watched him pick up both boxes with ease, noticed his muscles straining the sleeves of his T-shirt, Arianna felt anything but detached.

Moving here, living here, spending time with Sammy... Was it a huge mistake? She'd promised Chloe never to reveal the truth, had reiterated that promise when Chloe was dying. How could she go back on it?

Besides, revealing the truth might very well erase her new, tentative relationship with her son. If Jack knew about the huge secret she'd kept from him, he'd be furious. He might consider her character fatally flawed and refuse to let her see Sammy anymore. Which was his right; he was Sammy's father by adoption and by law.

But now that she'd gotten a taste of spending time with her son, she couldn't imagine giving up the privilege. More important than her own feelings, Sammy needed the help she could offer.

She just had to make sure to keep her distance from Jack. She liked him too much, but she didn't dare start to confide in him, to get close. No sense torturing herself.

They carried several more boxes and then paused at the same time, surveying the attic apartment. What to do next wasn't clear.

"Are you going to be okay living here? Looks like there's a lot of work to be done." Jack frowned at the remaining mess. "It would drive me crazy."

"Think where I've been staying," she said. "At least this mess is clean-up-able."

"You have a good attitude," he said, nodding approval.

It was the same thing Penny had said, and it shouldn't have warmed her as much as it did.

They carried one more load down. Penny stood beside an expensive sedan, talking to a man in a suit. They seemed to be arguing, and within a few seconds, the man threw up his hands, climbed into the car and drove away. Penny watched him go, then turned back toward the house. When she saw them, she shook her head and rolled her eyes. "I think I'm going to have to get out of here for a little bit," she said. "These men are driving me crazy."

"Is Branson Howe bugging you for a date?" Jack asked.

"Now, why would you say that?" Penny looked irritated.

"Because I think he's been trying to get up the courage to do that for a long time. You didn't shut him down, did you?"

"Yes, I did. I shut everyone down."

"You're breaking their hearts," Jack said.

"Don't you start." Penny bustled inside and came back with her purse and keys. "I'm serious. I'm leaving. I'm going to go see a woman friend, got that? A woman.

Because women are a lot more sensible than men." She climbed into her truck and drove off in a flurry of gravel.

Jack winced as he looked at Arianna. "I shouldn't have said anything. It's just that all the men in town talk about Penny. They're all thinking that it's been over a year since her divorce, and they can approach her now."

Arianna felt a stab of pain. Penny could start over, but she couldn't. Instead, she was living in a shabby, dirty place, as shabby and empty as her own life. Because she might have a good attitude in front of others, but in her heart, she knew an educated woman in her late twenties should have been doing a lot better.

There was a sound on the porch, a low whine. Arianna looked at Jack. "Did you hear that?"

"What's over there?"

They both hurried over and discovered a box, lined with a towel and holding one sad-looking, crying, cream-colored puppy. Arianna sank to her knees. "Oh, little guy, who left you here?"

Jack frowned in the direction that Branson's, and then Penny's, car had gone. "Could Branson have brought it?"

"I don't know him. Could he have?"

"He doesn't seem the type," Jack said. "More like the type who would arrange everything carefully."

"I wonder how long it's been here?" Gently, Arianna pulled the puppy out of the box and cuddled it close. Its little pink tongue licked her arm, and her heart melted. She looked up at Jack. "You know, this might be just what I need to make my house a home."

"No." He shook his head, hands on hips. "Animals aren't accessories."

"Well, I know that, silly," Arianna said. "But dogs are companions, and I'd take good care of it."

Jack sighed. "Let me run and check on Sammy, and then I'll take a look at him," he said. "He looks kind of young to be away from his mama."

"That's not good, right?" Arianna had heard that dogs needed to be with their mothers for the first eight weeks to learn good dog manners and be socialized properly.

"Right," Jack said. "There *is* a new mama out in the barn. In fact, she only has one pup, and he's about this one's age. Want to help me?" He smiled at her, and his whole face lit up, and Arianna's heart melted.

Which it shouldn't be doing. She needed to focus her affection on Sammy, and maybe a puppy. Not on Jack. Definitely not on Jack.

Chapter Five

After making sure the puppy was in no immediate distress, Jack hurried over to his house, caught the tail end of Sammy's session with his TSS and got instructions for following up. Then he grabbed Sammy and two bags of supplies—one for his son and one for the puppy.

As he carried Sammy over toward Penny's front porch, magpies scolded and mountain bluebirds twittered and swooped. The late-afternoon sun warmed his shoulders, and the weight of his son in his arms felt good and right.

Finally, he was starting to manage Sammy's condition, get him help and get their lives back on track.

Arianna sat on the top porch step, her auburn curls glowing like fire. She cradled the small, cream-colored puppy in her arms, talking softly to it.

The sight of Arianna's nurturing side tugged at his heart, and when she heard them coming and looked up, the warm glow in her eyes melted something inside him.

"I really want to keep him," she said.

"He's a cute little guy. Let me take a look." He set

down his bags and took the puppy from her, carefully, and she held out her arms for Sammy.

They worked well together. An automatic trade without words.

The puppy whined a little as Jack examined it, and Sammy turned his head to stare at the dog.

"He really noticed that." She patted Sammy's back. "See the puppy?"

"He notices animals more than he notices people," Jack said, and then he wished he hadn't.

Arianna looked up quickly. "That must be hard to deal with."

He nodded. "I'm used to it, but it makes me sad." He held up the puppy so Sammy could see it. "Dog," he said.

"See the dog?" Arianna added.

Sammy looked thoughtful but didn't speak.

"Does he know the word?"

"He used to," Jack said, and pain twisted his heart.

He met Arianna's eyes and saw a matching sorrow in hers.

The intimacy of their shared emotion felt too raw, and he looked away, focusing on the puppy. He examined eyes, ears, tail and paws. "He's healthy," he told her, "just too young to be left alone. That's why he's crying."

"Poor thing. I wonder what his story is."

Jack shook his head. "There are all kinds of reasons why a mother can't raise her pup," he said.

Arianna drew in a sharp breath, and when he looked up, her eyes glittered with unshed tears. Funny, he hadn't realized she was so sensitive. He put a hand on hers. "We'll find him a new mama," he reassured her.

She swallowed hard and nodded, and then Sammy started to fuss and the moment was over.

Half an hour later, at the barn, Jack inhaled the clean, lemony smell and smiled. "The volunteers keep this place really clean."

"It's staffed by volunteers? I thought the veterans cared for the dogs."

"It takes a village," Jack said. "Sometimes we don't have as many veterans, or they're working off-ranch, and then the community steps in to help."

The dogs started their usual uproar, and Sammy clapped his hands over his ears and started to cry.

"They'll quiet down in a minute," Jack told Arianna over the din. "Just bounce him, kind of hard." When she fumbled, he held out the puppy and they traded again.

Soon enough, the dogs quieted down and Sammy did, too. They walked down the aisle, and he could have predicted Arianna's reaction.

Puppy in hand, she knelt beside first one pen, then the next. She talked softly to the senior dogs, rubbed grizzled snouts, read the little cards on the front of each enclosure that told the dog's age, gender and something about them.

"Oh, look, Jack. This one's been here for over a year!" She studied the pit bull–rottweiler mix. "Why hasn't anyone adopted him?"

"We're not really so much about adoption, although we're thrilled when it happens," Jack said. "The veterans who stay here each pick out a dog to care for. Max is big, and he needs medication every morning and evening. He's a lot for anyone to handle, let alone a struggling veteran." Even as he said it, he knelt and reached into the pen to scratch behind the big black dog's ears. Normally he didn't let himself think too much about how long the dogs spent here or what their lives were like. As a veterinarian, he had to maintain some detachment.

Around Arianna, detachment was harder and harder to come by.

In Arianna's arms, the puppy started whining louder, causing Sammy to stare. Jack stood. "Come on, Buster," he said, spontaneously naming the pup. "Let's find you a mama, or at least, a mama for now."

The dog he'd been thinking of was at the end of the left-hand row of crates, and he hurried Arianna past the rest of the dogs on the line and knelt in front of the last pen. "Hey, Millie," he said gently.

The large beagle mix looked out at him with soulful eyes, her tail thumping.

"How's your pup doing, huh?" He opened the pen's door with one hand, still holding Sammy in the other. Millie was gentle beyond words and wouldn't dream of escaping or hurting anyone.

"Why does she only have one pup?" Arianna asked, kneeling beside the dog.

"Lots of possible reasons. She's old to be breeding, and she's had a lot of litters. That's why she was dropped off here. No use as a breeder anymore, and the owners were disgusted that she just had one pup."

"Well, I'm disgusted with them," Arianna said, rubbing the long, soft ears.

"It could be a blessing in disguise. She'll have plenty of extra milk, and her baby…" He nudged at the adorable pup sleeping beside her. "He's not had to compete for resources, so he's gentle as a lamb, too. What do you think, Millie? Can you take on another baby?"

Arianna held the whining puppy out, and the beagle let out a low woof, then sniffed him all over.

"You can put him down," Jack said. "I think she'll be nice."

Millie's pup lifted his head sleepily and then dropped it back down again. Millie licked the new, tiny pup all over, from head to toe, then nudged it toward her stomach. Soon the new baby latched on and began suckling with all its might.

Jack swallowed a lump in his throat. If only people could be as simple as animals, the world would be a better place. He glanced over at Arianna.

Her eyes were shiny again. "So sweet," she said, and then he noticed the tear running down her cheek. It was only natural for him to hold out an arm, bringing her into a hug. He wasn't sure why she let out a couple of sobs against his shirt, but hey…women, hormones, puppies… He rubbed his hand up and down her back.

After a moment she looked up at him, and he suddenly realized how close they were standing, how good her hair smelled and how wrong and forbidden it was to notice such things. He took a big step backward, forced out a laugh. "Well, that's our good deed for the day. Sammy and I have things to do. We'll see you tomorrow to get started figuring out nanny duties."

She didn't speak, and he didn't dare stay. He swung around and, God forgive him, he practically ran away, leaving her to find her way out of the barn and back to her apartment by herself.

Helping her just might prove too much, and too dangerous, for Jack.

The next morning, Arianna showed up at Jack and Sammy's house five minutes early—something of a record for her—only to find Jack with his jacket and shoes on, briefcase in hand. She blinked. "Am I late?"

"No, no. It's fine," he said. "I just need to give you some instructions before heading out."

Duly noted: on time for Jack meant at least ten minutes early.

She wasn't about to complain. She was still marveling over the blessing God had given her, allowing her to care for her son. She looked around and spotted Sammy, contentedly pushing blocks through holes on the top of a bin. Then she shed her own jacket and purse and pulled out her phone. "I'm going to record what you say, if that's okay," she said. "I don't want to make any mistakes."

He glanced over at her coat and purse. "Okay, first off, let's make sure that your purse is hung up out of Sammy's reach. I don't want him choking on small items or getting into medications. Even a little bit of aspirin or the like can make a baby sick."

She was already messing up. "Of course, I should have thought of that." She followed him to a closet where she could hang her things.

He brought her into the kitchen. "I know this is going to seem like overkill, but I have even more instructions than the last time, since you'll be with Sammy all day."

"It's fine. It's good." Her throat tightened unexpectedly. Jack was so careful, so thorough, at caring for Sammy. God had made sure Sammy was in a good home, that was for sure.

After walking her through the instructions and showing her where everything was kept—all in that flat, businesslike tone—Jack finally left. It felt like a relief.

Until she sat down with Sammy. "Hey, pumpkin," she said quietly.

He ignored her.

"Sammy?"

He continued pushing blocks into his bin. Or did he pause? She wasn't sure.

"Are you hungry?"

He looked up at her, a fleeting glance, and then back at his blocks.

"Daddy will come back," she said. "He always comes back."

No reaction there.

She blew out a sigh. These were going to be long days if she couldn't do even basic communication with Sammy. She was incredibly grateful for the opportunity, but it came accompanied by worry.

Problem solve. She'd claimed to know about autism when she'd asked Jack for the job, and she hadn't been lying. She needed to use that knowledge to help Sammy communicate. She couldn't freeze up just because he was her secret son.

She shook off her emotions and cast her mind back to the kids she'd worked with before, kids she'd cared for, a lot, but not with the depth of emotion she felt for Sammy.

A few of them had been nonverbal, although they'd managed to communicate through art.

She studied Sammy, thinking. Now that she was paying closer attention, she realized that he wasn't poking the blocks into the correct holes as she'd thought. Instead, he was putting all of them into the larger side hole, and struggling plenty to do that much.

Fine motor skills delay. It was typical, and no doubt his TSS workers would help him with it. In fact, maybe that was why he was playing with the blocks at all.

But it meant that having him express himself through art probably wasn't a good option.

Okay, she needed to try something else. She thought back to the kids she'd worked with and had a lightbulb moment: sign language.

That was something even young babies could learn. It didn't take a lot of coordination, nor verbalization skills.

She got on her phone and looked up "sign language" and "babies."

When Sammy stopped playing with the blocks and instead started banging one against his head, hard, she figured something was wrong. A check of the detailed schedule Jack had left confirmed that it was time for Sammy's midmorning snack.

She got out the whole-grain crackers Jack had told her to serve and handed Sammy one. He stuffed it into his mouth and then looked at her expectantly.

"Do you want more?" She put her thumbs against her fingertips, making her hands into ovals, and tapped them together. "More?"

Sammy stared.

Gently, she reached out and formed his hands into the same shape, then tapped them together. "More!" she said and handed him another cracker.

They went through the entire snack that way, and while she was still assisting him after his designated ten crackers, she thought she saw a glimmer of under-standing in his eyes.

Later in the day, she noticed he was looking at the door frequently. She found the sign for *daddy* on her phone. Then she found a photo of Jack and Sammy and brought it over to him. "Daddy," she said, pointing to Jack. Then she flattened her hand, splayed her fingers and tapped her forehead with her thumb. "Daddy. He'll be home soon."

She reached to help him, but he took the picture and grasped it in both hands, pulled it close to his face and stared at it.

Then he flattened his hand and tapped his forehead with his thumb. And looked at her.

Her heart expanded almost to bursting. He was smart! He *could* communicate. "That's right, Sammy!" she said and reached out to hug him, making it short and loose in deference to his likely preference for nonintense cuddling.

Indeed, he twisted away, but gently. Then he looked pointedly at the kitchen and made the "more" sign.

Arianna couldn't keep the smile off her face. He'd just asked for more food! And though it wasn't strictly his mealtime, she went and got him a bowl of fruit and more crackers. For him to communicate deserved a celebration.

They finished the snack together, and then she had Sammy sit with her in the kitchen while she made a modest dinner for him and his father. Pasta and cheese sauce with broccoli on the side. Cooking wasn't one of her duties, not officially, but she saw no reason not to help Jack out that way, since she was here all day.

A little later, Sammy looked at her with peculiar intent. He pointed at the picture of Jack and made the "daddy" sign. Then he pointed at Arianna and waited.

"He'll be home soon, buddy," she said.

He pointed at her again, and she stared at him. Could it be that he wanted to know the sign to use for her?

Before she could stop herself, she looked up the sign

for "mother." Five spread fingers, thumb tapped on the chin.

Should she teach her son to call her "mother"?

The temptation tugged hard at her. Who on Redemption Ranch, or in Esperanza Springs, would know what the sign meant? It could be her private little communication with her son.

But that would be wrong. She'd be using Sammy for her own selfish satisfaction. Throat tight, she punched the keys to look up the sign for "aunt." Make a close-fisted *A*, circle it beside the cheek a couple of times. It was a sweet sign.

She taught it to him, and he caught on quickly, his face lighting into something like a smile.

It was enough.

It would have to be enough.

"You're sure these colors are okay?" Arianna asked Penny several days later. She was unloading discount paint from her car and doubting herself. "I know you gave me free rein, but sometimes that's better in theory than in practice."

"Believe me, that's the least of my problems." Penny was carrying cans of paint from Arianna's car to the outdoor stairway that led to Arianna's apartment. "With Willie and Branson both bugging me for dates I don't want to go on, as well as running the ranch, I've got my hands full. Besides, your taste is better than most people I know."

"If you're sure." Arianna had a vision for the upstairs apartment, and she'd gotten a little carried away with it at the paint store.

Daniela Jiminez, one of the women who worked as a

therapist at the ranch, pulled up in her Jeep. "Did I hear there was a painting party out this way?"

"You sure did," Penny said and flashed a grin at Arianna. "I figured you might need some help. You don't mind, do you? I asked a couple of the other gals, too."

As if in response to her words, a truck pulled up. Kayla, who worked with Arianna in the church nursery, and Lily, who'd picked up those adorable twins, climbed out.

"Ready to work," Kayla said.

"I love painting," Lily added.

Their kindness warmed Arianna's heart. "You guys didn't have to do this. I'm sure you've got plenty to do at your own houses. And husbands and kids to take care of." In fact, all three of the other women—Daniela, Kayla and Lily—were relatively newly married. Both Kayla and Lily had kids, and Daniela had a suspiciously round belly.

"Oh, believe me, we welcome the chance to be away from our mom responsibilities for a little while," Lily said. "A girls' night is fun, even if it has to take place in the middle of the afternoon."

"And I brought chocolate." Daniela opened the passenger door of her Jeep and pulled out a tray of very fancy brownies. "To make up for the fact that I can't paint while I'm pregnant. I'm a whiz with masking tape in well-ventilated rooms, though."

Arianna inhaled the rich fragrance of them and regretfully patted her hips. "These jeans are already too tight. Don't tempt me."

"Jeans are made to be unsnapped," Lily said. "Besides, you have a beautiful figure. You have actual curves." She gestured at her own rail-thin self. "I dream of a figure like yours."

"Curves are beautiful," Daniela said, "or at least, that's what Gabe tells me." She blushed, and one hand rose to the scar on the side of her face.

Another vehicle, this one a giant SUV, sped up the long driveway and stopped in a flurry of gravel. A woman closer to Penny's age than Arianna's, wearing a Mountain Malamutes T-shirt, jumped out. "Am I late?"

"Yes, but it's okay." Penny hugged her and then introduced her to Arianna. "Thanks for coming, Marge. I know between the dogs and six kids, it's tough to get away."

"Tough, but welcome." Marge walked around, hugging the other women, then gripped Arianna's hand. "I'm real glad to meet you. Thanks for letting me in on your girls' night."

"Thank *you*," Arianna said, slightly overwhelmed by these women's willingness to help a near stranger.

They hauled the paint up the stairs and started spreading drop cloths and taping off the trim. "This is going to be so cute," Lily said. "I love the primary colors you chose. With a nice braided rug and the pine floors, it'll look great."

"You think so? I was afraid the bright blue and yellow would be too much."

"Bold but perfect," Lily declared, and the others nodded agreement.

They painted together for a couple of hours, making small talk. Arianna was impressed that they all worked hard. It wasn't their place, and they barely knew her, and yet they dug in and helped as if she were family.

"So how's it going with Jack?" Kayla asked as the afternoon light went golden. Then she slapped a hand over her mouth. "Sorry. I didn't mean to be nosy."

"But we're all curious, because he's seemed a little happier." Lily was pouring more paint into a roller tray.

"He was so unhappy before," Marge added. "With his wife."

"That's her sister!" Penny slapped Marge's arm gently. "Be nice."

"I'm sorry," Marge said. "Nobody ever knows what someone else is going through."

Jack had been unhappy with Chloe? That was the first Arianna had heard of it, and she doubted it was true. "It's okay, don't worry about it," she said. "Chloe was... Well, she was the perfect one out of the two of us. We didn't have a whole lot in common."

"Perfect, huh?" Penny raised an eyebrow.

"She wasn't perfect enough to forgive a rude remark like I just made to you," Marge said. "I was forever offending that woman. You seem a lot more relaxed."

"Um...thanks?" Arianna ran her brush carefully along the trim beside a window. "I just figure I don't have room to judge other people, that's all. But it's not Chloe's fault she was that way. Our parents were really, really rigid."

"Like Jack's," Marge said. "That must be why they got along so well."

Arianna thought back to Jack's father, sputtering in the coffee shop. He'd always seemed difficult to Arianna, making awkward comments and assumptions about young single women, and artists, and pretty much everything Arianna was. Jack's mother hadn't been as vocal, but she, too, had tended to judge first and ask questions later. And she'd seemed to particularly target Arianna.

"Chloe ran that True Love Waits club at our church

with an iron fist," Marge continued on. "Those teen girls were terrified of her."

Marge had her mouth open to continue talking, but at a glance from Penny, a subtle head shake, she shut it again.

Daniela leaned forward. "Did I hear right that you're teaching little Sammy some sign language?"

Arianna nodded, relieved at the change of subject. "It's really cute. He already understands the signs for *more* and *Daddy*."

"Oh, *more* was Leo's first word!" Kayla chuckled. "Kids. They're actually a little bit predictable."

"I think you're going to be really good for Sammy," Daniela said.

"And good for Dr. Jack," Marge added with a sly smile.

"Speaking of," Lily said, looking out the window. "He's coming this way with his adorable baby."

Arianna checked the time on her phone and clapped a hand to her forehead. "Guys, I have to take a break. I'm supposed to watch Sammy while Jack does some work with the rescue dogs out in the barn." She went out to the back porch-like area, a square with room for a chair and small table, surrounded by a railing.

Jack was trotting up the steps, the sun behind him adding gold to his light brown hair. He reached the top, not even winded, and smiled at her. "Ready for Sammy?"

"Yes, I'm sorry you had to bring him over." She had to keep better track of time if she was going to make a good impression as a nanny, good enough that Jack might let her stay awhile.

"No problem. I'll get my work in the barn done and then come back and get him so you can finish painting," he said. "I saw you made a meat loaf. You've been cooking for us all week, and I appreciate it. You should at least stay for dinner with us so you could benefit from your hard work."

An electric prickle raced up and down her spine. She didn't want to impose on Jack and Sammy's family time, nor establish a habit of being too close and personal. But if Jack were asking her to stay because he wanted her to...

"The therapists say it's good for him to witness interaction," Jack said. "If he's having dinner with us, and hears us talking and laughing, it might stimulate his own communication centers."

Arianna's face heated. How stupid of her to think Jack was interested in hanging out with her. "Oh, sure, if it's for Sammy." She glanced back into the kitchen, where the other ladies were working and, most likely, listening in. "I can have a quick dinner, but then I'm going to finish painting while it's still light. You guys go on home," she called back through the screen door. "You've been an amazing help, but I'm going to need to be gone a couple of hours."

"Go, go," Daniela said. "We'll just finish up what we're doing and let ourselves out."

She took Sammy from Jack's arms. "I've got you covered," she said. "We'll be hanging out at home." Then she felt stupid to have said that. Jack's house wasn't home, not to her.

He just gave her his usual sunny smile and trotted back down the steps.

She went back into the kitchen, where Sammy permitted some pats and cooing from the ladies before starting to fuss. Arianna gave each woman a quick hug. "Thanks so much, you guys. With all of you helping, it's almost done. I owe you big-time."

They all assured her they'd enjoyed it, and Daniela wrapped up a giant brownie for her to take along.

As she carried Sammy back to Jack's place, melancholy washed over her. She had loved the taste of community that she'd gotten with those women. She would love to build on those friendships.

Except how real were the friendships when nobody knew the truth about her?

If they knew that Sammy was actually her son, she was fairly certain they'd all despise her. As would Jack. And unfortunately, she couldn't avoid spending more and more time with him, it seemed. Time when she needed to be on her guard, to make sure the truth didn't slip out. Starting with their cozy family dinner tonight.

Chapter Six

When Jack walked into his house after working in the barn with the dogs, the first thing he saw was Arianna, stirring something in a pot on the stove. Her wild curls were back in a ponytail, at least mostly, and her cheeks were flushed. She was humming.

In the doorway between the kitchen and the hall, Sammy bounced contentedly in his jumper. The smell of meat loaf and onions and potatoes made Jack's mouth water.

He stopped for a moment just to take it in, this unfamiliar, deep feeling: *I'm home. This is home.*

He must have made some noise, because she turned, and her wide smile made her even prettier. "Oh, hey, glad you're home," she said.

Did she hear how domestic that sounded? Could she be feeling anything similar to what he was feeling?

Probably not. It was probably just wishful thinking on his part.

After all, what did he know about having a loving family? His own mom had usually looked angry at this time of day, because someone was late or unappreciative or inappropriately dressed for dinner.

"I should go shower," he said. Chloe would have already waved him upstairs, grimacing. Working with animals meant he picked up a little bit of their fur and smell even if he'd just been doing quick exams, as he had this afternoon.

Arianna lifted her hands, palms up. "Don't worry about it. Just wash up in the kitchen sink—it's your house." She stepped closer. "And you don't smell too terribly doggy," she said with a grin.

She smelled good, like flowers.

Jack swallowed and took a step back and looked around the kitchen. Arianna had laid out plates and cutlery on the plank table in the kitchen. Sammy's high chair was there, in between the two set places. Ketchup and salad dressing were set out in their original bottles, and the napkins were paper, although neatly folded.

He thought about his parents, their formal style of dining. Chloe had loved it, had loved going to their house and eating well-prepared food on their fine china.

Obviously, Arianna wasn't much for formal dining. Or she wasn't going to try to make it happen at the end of a workday with a hungry baby.

He liked that.

Confused by his feelings, he strode over to the doorway and knelt in front of Sammy. He was delighted when his son held out a hand to him, and he picked Sammy up and swung him high. Sammy didn't chortle like a lot of babies would, but his expression changed, his mouth quirking up a little and then opening.

"He's loving it!" Arianna stood, watching and smiling. "Look at that happy face."

More emotions nudged at Jack's heart, emotions that made him uncomfortable. Undeniably, he and Arianna were on the same wavelength. He drew in a breath and, after one more swing, took Sammy to his high chair.

"Thanks for staying for dinner," he said. "I should have thought about the fact that you're still commuting to your aunt and uncle's place. I hope this won't make your drive down the mountain too difficult."

"It's fine," she said as she carried a big bowl of salad to the table. "Truthfully, I'm glad to have a nice meal in a clean place."

Jack thought of her aunt and uncle's home, how messy and disorganized it had been. "It must have been hard for you, living there."

"Oh no, don't get me wrong," she said quickly. "My uncle and aunt have been fabulous to me. I'm so grateful that they let me stay with them this long. Could you grab the potatoes?" she added, nodding toward the steaming bowl. She tipped the meat loaf, draining the grease into an empty can, and then carefully put slices onto a plate. "There," she said as she carried it to the table. "All of this can cool while you say a blessing."

"Sure," Jack said, even though he hadn't prayed publicly in a long time. They each took one of Sammy's hands, and then there was an awkward hesitation before he reached out and trapped her fingers in his. Long and slender, with calluses. Just as he'd imagined. He cleared his throat. "Father God, we thank You for this food and the chance to enjoy it together." He was about to summon up more to say when Sammy let out a series of bleating sounds, his usual signal for hunger.

"In Christ's name, amen," Jack said quickly, and when he opened his eyes, Arianna was smiling.

"Short prayers are the best kind sometimes," she said, and he laughed and nodded.

She insisted on serving, which gave him a few minutes to look around the kitchen. Of course, it was messy. This was Arianna, and she'd been taking care of Sammy as she cooked.

But he also noticed that she had put up the curtains he'd had sitting in their package for weeks and hung a small painting he didn't remember seeing before on the wall above the table. "You did some decorating."

"I hope you don't mind," she said as she handed him a steaming plate. "It just seemed like you needed little bit of… I don't know…"

"A woman's touch? Yes. We do."

She was looking at him while he said that, and something flashed in her eyes. He would have given a lot to know what it meant.

But it wasn't his business to go digging into her psyche. He needed to keep his distance. He busied himself with cutting Sammy some small pieces of meat and potatoes, and Sammy ate with a surprising amount of enthusiasm. "Wow, he seems to like it."

"I was hoping he would. I noticed he's a little picky about texture."

"Soft, but not too soft," he said. "This is perfect."

"For him. Sorry I made you baby food."

"No, this is really good," Jack said, meaning it. He scooped in several more bites before continuing, "I love comfort food, and your sister never made it."

Silence.

Jack replayed what he'd said in his mind and then felt like a complete jerk. He shouldn't be making comparisons. He shouldn't speak ill of the dead.

After a moment Arianna spoke, her voice more thoughtful than condemning. "Chloe was more like our mom, who really wanted to be sophisticated about food," she said. "She was a wannabe foodie."

"So that's where Chloe got it," he said, relieved that she had ended the awkwardness. "What about you?"

"Oh, I was a disappointment. I was always so ordinary." She laughed dismissively.

Oh no, Arianna. You're anything but ordinary.

Even the thought made guilt overwhelm him. Arianna might not know it, but Chloe had been pathologically jealous about Jack and other women—for no reason Jack could understand—and her jealousy had focused on her sister. Chloe had suspected that Jack was drawn to Arianna. That was one big reason she had pushed her sister away. And it was one reason Jack had always tried to keep his distance from Arianna. He didn't want to stir Chloe's anger or give her any cause at all to feel more jealous.

Now Chloe's frequent disapproval echoed in his mind.

What was he doing, having Arianna in his house, in the mother's role, having a family dinner?

Unfortunately, Chloe had shared her belief that Jack was attracted to Arianna with his parents, with whom she was quite close. And considering how negatively Jack's father had reacted to them having coffee together, if he heard that they'd shared a home-cooked dinner, say, it would create a big uproar.

Jack could deal with his father, but Arianna shouldn't have to. Dad was blunt, sometimes rude. He could hurt Arianna. That was the last thing Jack wanted.

Oblivious to Jack's inner turmoil, Arianna was spooning bites of meat loaf into Sammy's mouth. She glanced over at Jack. "Look, he's starting to eat with a spoon a little bit," she said. "The next step will be to have him hold it himself. I've been reading about breaking everything down into small steps, and the TSS who was here yesterday helped me figure it out."

Mixed feelings coursed through Jack. Arianna was warm. She was wonderful with Sammy. He'd done the right thing hiring her.

Except that he liked her way too much. Admired her. Could fall for her.

He stood and started clearing off the table, aware that it seemed abrupt but unable to sit still a moment longer. He brought a cloth over to the table and wiped Sammy's face. Then he nodded at Arianna's still half-full plate.

"I'll take Sammy up to his bath and bed," he said. "That will give you a chance to finish your dinner in peace."

But as he picked Sammy up, Arianna pushed her plate away. "Do you mind if I come with you?"

As she tagged along to the bathroom, as she watched Jack kneel to gently wash Sammy, ignoring the fact that he was getting soaked himself, Arianna swallowed the tight knot in her throat.

She was absolutely blessed among women to be able to participate in her son's care. To watch his loving father bathe him, to help put him to bed.

She didn't deserve it. How well she knew that. God had given her grace.

Jack had gone quiet, but that was okay. Sammy liked quiet and peace. So did Arianna, for that matter. She handed Jack the hooded towel that hung on the back of the door, and he pulled Sammy out and wrapped him in it.

Sammy almost smiled, and Arianna's heart melted at the sight of Jack holding his son in such a loving way.

If there were ever any question about whether adoptive parents could care for their children as much as biological parents did, it was answered in this tender moment. Jack clearly adored his son. And although Sammy wasn't expressive, the way he stared up at his father, his focus and intensity, made Arianna believe that he adored Jack just as much.

God works all things for good.

Tears pushed at the backs of her eyes as she followed the father and son into Sammy's room. She was tired, that was all. Like every day, she'd gotten up early to take a stab at cleaning her aunt's kitchen, and then she'd driven up the mountain. She'd been working with Sammy most of the day and then painting in what little time off she had.

That had to be the reason she was emotional. She wasn't getting enough sleep. She was tired.

"Pick him out a pair of pajamas," Jack said as he sat on the edge of the rocking chair, Sammy bundled in the towel in his arms.

So Arianna knelt and opened the drawer of Sammy's cute, pale blue dresser. She stared in amazement at the folded pajamas lined up perfectly in the drawer. Wow, Jack was neat. "Is there a particular pair he really likes?"

"The blue ones with teddy bears. They're the softest."

So she pulled them out and helped Jack diaper Sammy and then put him into the one-piece pajamas. Sammy rubbed the backs of his little hands over his eyes.

"Somebody's tired," Jack said. Tenderly, he set

Sammy down in the crib and rubbed his arms and legs with gentle pressure. "It helps relax him," Jack explained. "Helps him drift off to sleep."

Hesitantly, Arianna reached in and did the same, rubbing her fingers gently along Sammy's pajama-clad arms and legs.

What would it be like if this were real? If Jack was the father and she was the mother and Sammy was their child?

She already knew: it would be all she'd ever wanted in the world.

But no way, no way could she have it, and she was going to break her own heart if she kept having these crazy fantasies. She coughed, trying to clear her throat of the golf ball–size lump that had lodged there. "I think I'm going to go downstairs, give you two some privacy," she said in a rush. She backed out of the room, and then, at the doorway, she spun and hurried down the stairs, her feet clattering. She'd probably woken Sammy up again, just when Jack was getting him to sleep, but it was better than falling apart in front of Jack and then trying to explain it.

She went into the bathroom, locked the door, sank down on the edge of the bathtub and turned on the fan and the water. Then she let the sobs come.

How had she ever given her precious baby away? Why, oh, why had she done it?

Intellectually, of course, she knew that it had been the right thing to do. She believed in adoption, and she'd read all the research showing that parental love in an adoptive family was just as strong as parental love in a biological family. Sometimes better if a biological parent wasn't ready.

But what the literature hadn't said was how much it could hurt the birth mother. How the thought, let alone the sight and sound and smell, of the child she'd grown in her own body could tug her heart straight out of her chest.

Arianna had been drifting through life ever since she'd given birth, and this was why. Because there was a hole in her. Because she felt incomplete and didn't know if that would ever change. Because she was grieving the fact that she couldn't see her son, spend the days with him, get to know him, watch his every move.

She heard Jack's heavy tread on the stairs, and it brought her back to reality. She was in a better position than a lot of birth mothers, because she'd placed her child with family. And now she *did* get to help with Sammy. She did get to know him, at least some, and she could see for herself that he was fine, doing well. It was more than she had ever expected, because it was more than Chloe would ever have permitted. It was more than many birth mothers had, and it would have to be enough.

She splashed water on her face and ran her fingers through her hair. Maybe, in the dimming light of evening, Jack wouldn't notice that she'd been crying.

But when she came out of the bathroom, he was standing in the middle of the living room waiting for her. He studied her face, tilting his head to one side. "You okay?"

She nodded quickly. "Fine," she said, afraid to say any more. She hurried into the kitchen, started gathering up her things. "I hate to leave you with this mess," she said to him when he followed her. "Just let it go and I'll clean it up tomorrow."

"You're already doing enough for us," he said. "Besides, you know I like to clean."

Even in the midst of her distress, that made her smile. "You're strange," she said.

"In a bad way?" His tone was light, but his gaze lingered on hers.

She licked her lips. "I better get going," she said nervously.

"I feel terrible about having you drive down the mountain," he said. "Why don't you just stay up here tonight?"

His offer seemed to hang in the air between them. What was he actually suggesting? Why was he looking at her that way? And why was her own heart beating so fast?

She reached for her newfound faith and values. "Jack, I would never... That's not what I do." She was about to say more, to describe the change she'd gone through.

But he held up a hand as color climbed from his neck into his face. "I didn't mean that the way it sounded," he said, his words tumbling over each other. "I just meant, I hate to have you drive so late at night. I'm sure you could stay with Penny."

"No, no," she said. "I have to go. I need to go home. I'll be fine." She headed toward the door. When she went to open it, he was there, opening it and holding it for her.

He was so close that she could smell his spicy, masculine scent.

He stared down at her and lifted his hand. One finger brushed her cheek.

She drew in her breath with a gasp. He was going to kiss her. And God forgive her, but she was going to let him.

But something came into his eyes and he pulled back, his expression disconcerted. "Go get in your car," he said, his voice rough. "I'll watch you."

"Jack…"

"Go on. Now." It was an order.

And there was something in his eyes, some wildness that she had never seen in her gentle brother-in-law. She spun and scurried to her car, her heart pounding so hard that it made her breathless.

Chapter Seven

Two days later, Jack still felt like an idiot.

He had gotten carried away when Arianna had stayed for dinner, acted ridiculous. He'd behaved like a boy-friend, not a former brother-in-law and an employer, and it was inappropriate and wrong.

It wasn't possible that he was attracted to Arianna. It had just been the emotions caused by having her there for a homey dinner. Her love of Sammy, the home-cooked meal, the sunset…all of it had contributed to a romantic feeling, and he had let himself go there when he shouldn't have.

Ever since, his emotions had been in such turmoil that avoiding Arianna had felt like a necessity. Yester-day he'd managed to keep his distance aside from a few instructions in the morning and a quick handoff of Sammy in the evening.

But today, Willie had driven his truck down to town to help Arianna bring her few things up to move into the new apartment.

Now she, Penny and Willie were carrying boxes up the outdoor stairway that led to her apartment.

Jack was young and able-bodied, more so than Willie, and what kind of gentleman would let ladies and an old man do a bunch of lifting and hauling?

He had to help. Even though he sensed that her moving in was going to be a disaster.

He'd help because it was the right thing to do, and then he'd stay away. She didn't work for him on Saturdays and Sundays, and there was no reason for him to be around her, not at all. After a half hour of carrying boxes, he'd leave Arianna alone for the rest of the weekend.

He picked Sammy up and parked him on his hip. Sammy was still sleepy and leaned his shampoo-smelling head against Jack's shoulder.

This is for him.

Arianna was great with Sammy, and for his son's sake, Jack could handle her presence. Even though he was attracted, he didn't have to act on it.

As soon he'd crossed the yard, Penny came over and held out her arms, Willie right behind her. "Let me hold that sweet baby while you help carry boxes," she said.

Sammy went to her willingly, and she tickled his chin. "You see what I did there," she said to Willie, laughing. "Now I get to chill out with this beautiful boy."

Willie gave her a tender smile. "If it were up to me, you'd sit in the shade and relax all the time."

Penny blushed.

Leaving them to what looked an awful lot like flirting, Jack strode over to the truck, picked up a couple of boxes—one coming open, the other ripped on one side—and carried them upstairs, shaking his head. Ariana had probably packed at the last minute, like she seemed to do most things.

When he walked into the apartment, the sight that greeted him made him stop still.

Arianna was shoving a chair to one corner of the main room. Sunlight glinted on her hair, turning it into a fiery mane as she tilted her head to one side, studying the effect. Then she spun around, found an empty box and set it beside the chair as if it were an end table. She rummaged through another box, found a large scarf and draped it over the box. Suddenly, the little corner looked cozy, a nice place to curl up with a book.

Something tightened inside him. Arianna had a passion for beauty and color, and she was so creative. So different from him—opposite, really. Maybe that was why he found her fascinating.

To cover his reaction, he cleared his throat as he set down the boxes he was carrying, then crossed his arms as she turned to him. "You went pretty outrageous with the wall color," he said, looking around.

"Outrageous?" She lifted an eyebrow as she turned a slow 360, studying the walls, three blue and one yellow. "I wondered if it was too much, but Penny seems to like it and so did the ladies. They finished all my painting the other night while I was with you." The color in her cheeks heightened, and she looked away. "Wasn't that nice of them?"

"It *was* nice. They're good people." *And it gave you the chance to hang around with me and Sammy, like you were part of the family.* Remembering the domestic evening they'd spent together made Jack feel a little warm, too.

And those were thoughts he didn't need to be thinking, feelings he didn't need to be having. "I'll, um, run up the rest of the boxes if you'd like to keep setting up."

After that, he'd take Sammy back to his house, where he felt a little more in control.

As he was bringing up the last load of boxes—surprising that Arianna had so few possessions—Penny and Willie followed, Penny carrying Sammy.

"There's my little man," Arianna cooed.

He glanced back from where he was setting down the boxes in time to see Arianna leaning toward Sammy, smiling and gently rubbing his arm. Sammy rocked a little and vocalized, an *ah-ah-ah* sound Jack hadn't heard him make in a long time.

"Such a cutie," Penny said, and Willie reached out a finger to tickle Sammy's neck, making him half flinch, half giggle.

That warm feeling in Jack's heart as he watched was unfamiliar, but he knew what it was: family.

Penny and Willie and Arianna felt like family. And they were a lot more affectionate than his own family had ever been.

But he had to be careful. Penny and Willie were fine, they'd most likely stay around. But Arianna was here temporarily. She obviously wasn't the "put down roots" type, if the few boxes that constituted her possessions were any indication.

Best not to let that family feeling penetrate too deeply in regards to Arianna. Yes, she was Sammy's aunt, but she was a free spirit and would probably just be in and out of his life.

"I can help you unpack your kitchen stuff," Penny said to Arianna.

Arianna did a mock cringe. "I, um, actually don't have any."

"How have you managed to cook for yourself?" Jack blurted out.

She shrugged. "I've mostly been renting rooms in friends' houses or furnished places," she said. "There never was a need. It's okay. I can pick up some stuff in the next few weeks."

"Or this one could take you to town to get some stuff, and pick up your car, too," Willie suggested, nodding at Jack.

"Oh, that's not really necessary." Arianna looked uneasy.

Of course she did. He'd come on pretty strong when they were last alone together.

"Penny and I will watch the baby," Willie went on. "And Jack would probably even advance you the money from your first paycheck." Willie nudged him.

Arianna glanced quickly at Jack, as if to see whether that was true.

She was broke and she needed some basics to survive. He couldn't leave her to make do without a pan or cup or plate to her name, could he?

Willie leaned closer to Jack. "Gives me a little more time with Penny," he whispered. "And I figured it might be a good thing for you young people, too."

Great, Willie was matchmaking. "Penny," Jack said with a feeling of desperation, "you probably have a ton of other stuff to do, right?"

She shrugged. "More important than taking care of this little peanut? Not hardly. Go on, go."

"I could use a few things from the general store," Arianna said hesitantly, "and I need a ride down to my car. But I don't want to put you out."

"It won't put me out," he said, giving in to the forces

pushing him into a shopping date with Arianna. A shopping date brimming full of forbidden fruit.

Oh no. Not Donegal's Hardware.

Arianna didn't move to exit Jack's truck as he pulled into one of the diagonal parking spots in front of the hardware store that had supplied the town with wrenches and mousetraps and road salt as long as she could remember.

"I might do better at one of the big-box stores out on the highway," she said to Jack. "I need a little bit of everything, and I don't think the hardware store has it all."

"You'll be surprised at what they've done to the place," Jack said. "It's not Donegal's Hardware anymore, even though most townspeople still call it that. It's Donegal's General Store, and they have a little bit of everything."

She sat still in the truck, trying to figure out how to escape and whether she needed to. But Jack had come around and was opening her door, and that distracted her. When did a guy do that, except on a date? She flushed, ignored the hand he extended and climbed out.

"Who's running the store now?" she asked. "Surely not Mr. and Mrs. Donegal?"

He shook his head. "Old Mr. Donegal passed away, but Mrs. Donegal is still there sometimes. Her daughter-in-law, Courtney, is the one who really runs the place."

Arianna's heart started thumping, slow and heavy, even as she tried to calm herself. The Donegals didn't know anything, she reminded herself. As long as she could stay calm, everything would be okay.

They walked inside, and it was like the old Donegal's Hardware, but different. There were the same bins of nails and extension cords and the faintly chemical smell of fertilizer and weed killer. From the back of the store came the grinding sound of someone making a key. Sweet, soft memories of simpler times assailed her.

But it wasn't the same. Nothing stayed the same. The store was bigger now, with a candy counter, displays of home goods and even some clothing.

"They knocked out a wall and took over the soda fountain next door," Jack said, gesturing toward the far side of the store, where a row of turquoise-covered stools sat along a counter lined with napkin holders and salt and pepper shakers.

Jack led the way toward an aisle with a sign proclaiming it held kitchen supplies. "Courtney's husband, Malachi, is still a professor at the community college," he explained. "And did you know their son, Nathan? Real smart guy. I heard he's teaching at the University of Colorado. Chemistry, I think."

Hearing Nathan's name on Jack's lips caused a flutter in Arianna's stomach, but she was relieved to learn that Nathan was living up north and doing well. *Breathe*, she told herself. *Everything's going to be fine.*

At least, as fine as it could be with the secrets she guarded in her heart.

There was Hannah Johnson from the bakery, buying mousetraps. "You didn't see me with these," she said with mock sternness. "Preventative measures. That's all."

"Just keep making your cinnamon muffins, and my lips are sealed," Jack said.

One of the store's workers called out a greeting, and Jack waved back. "How's school, Marla?" he asked.

"I'm loving it," she said. "Photography is my life."

She glanced around quickly and added, "After Donegal's General, of course."

Arianna looked at the pots and pans and selected an inexpensive skillet and pot. The initial expense was going to be tough to cover, but she'd be able to eat much more cheaply if she cooked, and healthily, too.

"Chloe used to love these," Jack said, holding up a heavier pan.

"Yeah, well, Chloe could afford it," she said and then bit her lip.

Jack was looking at her quizzically. "Does it bother you when I mention her?"

"No. No, it's good. And I didn't mean to sound bitter, not at all. I'm glad she had all the nice things, since they meant a lot to her."

"They did," Jack said, and their eyes met for the briefest moment. But it was enough to read a meaning: Jack wasn't the type to care much about material things.

Neither was Arianna. But the last thing she needed was to focus on what she and Jack had in common.

"I wish I hadn't gotten rid of so much," Jack said. "The church was helping a family whose home burned down, and I just boxed up a lot of Chloe's cookware that I'd never use myself and drove it over." A shadow passed across his face, and Arianna could imagine why.

A lot of people coped with loss by clinging to the loved one's stuff, but Jack wasn't that type. He'd want to clean up and move on.

"I can't afford a set of heavy-duty cookware," she said quietly. "Anyway, I like to travel light."

Jack studied her. "If it's a question of how much I'm willing to advance your salary, it's whatever you need.

Don't let money keep you from getting what you need to be comfortable."

"Thanks," she said, wondering why he was being so generous. Was it just his nature, would he do the same for any employee or was he treating her differently because she was Chloe's sister? "I appreciate it. I'll get what I need, but these—" she held up the lightweight skillet and pot "—these are fine."

He hesitated, then asked, "How come you've lived like that, traveling light? It seems like the opposite of what Chloe wanted."

No need to tell Jack that the reason she'd stopped thinking about the future, that she'd never wanted to settle anywhere, was that she'd given up her precious baby for adoption. When she'd done that, she'd given up her dreams of a home, as well. "We're—we were—pretty different." *Leave it at that.*

"Chloe was so keen on making a home, trying to have it warm the way you guys didn't have growing up." He picked up a couple of serving utensils and dropped them into the basket. "I hope you don't mind my saying that. I know your parents could be sort of…" He trailed off.

"Cold and judgmental?"

"Yeah. That's pretty much how Chloe felt, and even though I didn't see them often, I got that vibe from them. Do you like these?" He thrust a purple pot holder set into her hands. "I guess that's why Chloe and I understood each other. We grew up a similar way."

She nodded as she took the pot holder set out of his hands and set it back on the shelf. There wasn't much else to say about her family of origin, and truth to tell, she was surprised Chloe had revealed so much to Jack, even surprised Chloe had experienced their parents that way. She'd always come so much closer to meeting their exacting standards than Arianna had.

Of course, Chloe had tried a lot harder. And the stress of that had taken its toll in all kinds of ways.

After they'd gathered a few more things Arianna needed, and Jack had insisted on paying for them—which, however embarrassing, definitely helped, but she made sure to reiterate that he should take the balance out of her first paycheck—Jack stopped in the middle of carrying things out to the car. "You know what I'm hungry for?"

"What?" She lifted her eyes to his strong jaw and handsome face and then looked as quickly away. Not things she should focus on.

"A hot-fudge sundae," he said. "And they make really good ones here at Donegal's. They'll even give you extra fudge if you ask. Want one?"

Yum. Stress eating was her downfall, always had been. "Don't tempt me," she said.

"They're really good. They have small ones, if you're not super hungry, but I'm getting a large. Come on." He took her hand and tugged her toward the soda fountain side of the place.

She followed, the feel of his work-calloused hand stealing her breath. She didn't normally think of a veterinarian as doing physical work, but Jack trimmed horses' hooves and birthed calves. A country veterinarian relied on his own strength, and Jack had plenty.

They sat next to each other on stools that seemed to be placed just a little too close together. She could feel the warmth of his jeans-clad thigh next to hers, and suddenly, she was finding it hard to breathe.

"The usual, Dr. Jack?" The woman behind the counter sounded amused.

"Two of them," he said and then turned to Arianna. "That is, if double hot fudge on coffee ice cream sounds at all good to you."

"Don't forget the whipped cream and extra nuts," the server said.

Arianna's restraint lasted at least three seconds. "Okay. I'll have one, too."

"Arianna Shrader!" The high, raspy voice behind her went right down Arianna's spine and back up again. She turned and half stood to face a hunched, white-haired woman leaning on a cane.

She'd aged more than Ariana would have expected in just a couple of years, and it squeezed Arianna's heart. She'd always liked Nathan's grandmother. She leaned in and kissed the woman's dry, powdery cheek. "Hey, Mrs. Donegal."

Mrs. Donegal gave her a surprisingly fierce hug, then released her and waved a hand at Jack, who'd stood when she'd approached. "I see you all the time, but this girl's like the prodigal daughter. How have you been, honey?"

"Good. Doing art therapy," she said, blinking a little.

"That boy made a big mistake when he let you go," Mrs. Donegal declared. "You know, he's never found another." She looked sharply at Jack. "Are you two dating?"

"No!" Arianna said, her face heating.

"Not at all," Jack said at the same time.

"Well, good. Because I don't mind saying I'd like to see Nathan settle down with someone like you. Maybe you could pull him back here where he belongs."

Jack cleared his throat. "I heard he was doing something important at the University of Colorado," he said.

"That's right," old Mrs. Donegal said, her face visibly lifting. "Working on a fertilizer that'll double crop production, and they want to use it somewhere in Africa. Help people get more out of their land." She sighed. "Oh, I know he's a different one, and he says he's perfectly happy being single, but I just don't know. I'm afraid he gets lonely."

"Here you go." Two hot-fudge sundaes appeared in front of them, brought not by their original server, but by Courtney Donegal, Nathan's mother. "Hey, Arianna, good to see you. Mom, stop trying to find Nathan a woman. He's doing fine. Doing the work he loves. He and Arianna were never serious."

She ought to speak up, agree, laugh, congratulate them on Nathan's success. And she *was* happy for Nathan, and not surprised he'd done so well.

It was just the enormity of discussing him with Jack here.

Fortunately, Jack carried the conversation, asking about Nathan, encouraging them to brag, which gave Arianna a chance to regain her composure.

Wasn't his success evidence that she'd done the right thing, not telling Nathan about her pregnancy? He was following his calling, making a difference, using that mighty, impressive mind of his.

"Come on, Mother. Let them eat their sundaes before they melt," Courtney said firmly, taking her mother-in-law's arm and leading her away. "It was good to see you both. Enjoy."

Arianna stared at the giant sundae in front of her so she wouldn't have to look at Jack. Some women's appetites would have been demolished by a stressful encounter with an ex's family.

Not Arianna. The sundae looked fantastic.

"Dig in," Jack said. He stuck his spoon into the ice cream, took a bite and smiled, the pleasure going all the way up to his eyes.

Arianna swallowed. Wow. Hastily, she looked down at the sundae and took a bite of creamy richness.

"Good, isn't it?" he asked, and they focused on their food for several blissful moments.

"You know, Chloe would never slow down enough to enjoy a sundae with me," he said, and then, when she looked up at him, he covered her hand with his, giving it a quick squeeze. "I'm sorry I keep talking about her. It's just that you look like her, I guess, and make me think of her."

"I understand." She put down her spoon with her sundae half-finished. "Chloe had a lot of self discipline, unlike me. That's why she was able to stay so thin."

Jack frowned. "Even when she wanted to gain some weight to try to get pregnant, she couldn't make herself relax and eat more." He shook his head. "I've always wondered whether stress was a factor in her getting that blood clot. They say it wasn't, but…still, I wonder if there was something I could have done differently to help her, maybe avoid that fate."

"I've wondered the same thing," Arianna admitted. "I wish I spent more time with her, with you guys." It would have been painful, but if only they'd been able to work through that, maybe she could have lightened Chloe's load, helped her cope.

Jack nodded, his face grave.

She'd always wondered what Chloe had told him

about Arianna, if she'd ever shared reasons for the obvious fact that they didn't get along.

"I know God has a plan," he said finally, "but sometimes, it's hard to fathom."

"We'll understand someday. Chloe does now, I'm sure." Because despite all her issues, Chloe had been a believer, strong in her faith.

"It's good we can talk about it together." Jack gave her a warm smile. "I'm glad you're here, Arianna."

Their gazes met. She couldn't look away.

Until a tall man approached them from behind. "Arianna? Listen, I just got into town. Haven't even checked in with the family yet, but I'd heard you were living here now. I was hoping to see you."

A prickle of doom crackled through Arianna's body. "Hi, Nathan," she said.

Chapter Eight

"You sure you're okay?" Jack asked Arianna two hours later, as they walked slowly toward the barn. Jack was carrying Sammy on his shoulders. He probably should have left Sammy with Penny for another hour while he did the required vet checks on the dogs, but he wanted to maximize his time with his son on the weekend. He'd figured that Arianna would see his need for assistance and offer to help, because that was the type of person she was. He'd been right, and he was glad. Because he also wanted to spend a little more time with Arianna on this warm summer Saturday.

He wanted to find out more about her relationship with Nathan.

As they opened the barn door, the dogs registered their presence with barks and howls and yelps, high and low and everything in between.

"Jack, he's not putting his hands on his ears!" Arianna said, her voice excited. "Oh, well, wait, there he goes. But he listened to the noise for a few seconds first."

He smiled at her enthusiasm. "We take what progress we can get."

He moved ahead into the barn, checking on a couple of dogs, an ear infection and a dog recovering from being spayed. Arianna wandered around with Sammy, kneeling to show him various dogs, talking in a gentle, upbeat voice.

What had been her relationship with the brilliant Nathan? What was it now?

Had the talented, nerdy professor broken her heart?

He didn't like the idea of it. And he was her brother-in-law, the closest thing she had to a male relative. Who better to offer her support and protection?

He came out of the second pen and knelt beside her and Sammy. True to form, Sammy had discovered a stick and was beating it on the front of a pen. The old dog inside didn't seem to mind.

"Did Nathan want to see you again?" he asked quietly.

She glanced at him and then focused on Sammy, tugging up his little jeans and straightening his sweatshirt.

Jack tried again. "I don't think I even knew you were dating him. Was that during the summer you spent here?"

She nodded, still not looking at him.

"Was it a serious relationship?"

Rather than answering, she rose to her feet and grasped Sammy's hand. "Let's go look at the mama and pups," she said, tugging Sammy along. She held him by his hands, encouraging him to walk.

Briefly, Jack was distracted by his son's heels-up, halting gait. Sometimes he noticed things that made him think Sammy didn't have autism. That gait, though, was a sign that he did.

Arianna was distinctly ignoring him. "Look," he said, "if you don't want to talk about Nathan…"

"Isn't that pretty obvious?" She continued to back away, holding Sammy's hands, all smiles for his son.

The idea of Arianna having a boyfriend, back then or now, did strange things to Jack. He had no right at all to feel possessive, but he most certainly did feel that way.

It was just that a guy like Nathan wasn't right for Arianna. She was creative, fun, a little wild. Nathan was dead serious, the type to spend every free moment at work.

He tried one more time. "If Nathan bothers you, let me know."

She met his eyes then, and to his surprise, hers were brimming with tears. Automatically, he stepped forward, reached to touch her shoulder. "You're upset. I'm sorry."

"No, it's fine. I'm fine." She stopped in front of the pen that held the mother and pups and reached up to open it. The new puppy stumbled out in cute, awkward puppy style.

"Look, Sammy, a puppy!" Arianna's voice was uncharacteristically shrill.

Sammy waved a hand toward the animal, batting at it. The puppy latched onto his tiny hand and gnawed with sharp puppy teeth.

Sammy wailed.

"You have to be careful with him around a puppy!" Jack whisked Sammy away.

"I'm sorry," she said as Jack checked Sammy's hand and then bounced him in the vigorous way that he liked.

Slowly, Sammy's cries subsided.

Jack's thoughts were in turmoil. Arianna was in tears because of Nathan. If the man came up here to see her, could he handle that? Would it be good or bad for Sammy?

And what was this powerful jealousy he was feeling?

He gave Sammy to Arianna. Quickly, he checked the two puppies and the mama dog, then gathered the few things they'd brought up and led the way back down to the house.

Given his weird feelings, the last thing he should do was to invite Arianna to come in. He felt as if an inner judge was setting a boundary. The judge's face morphed from Chloe's to his mother's to his father's and back again.

He couldn't start anything up with Arianna, not without playing into every one of their suspicions.

But Arianna looked sad, a little lost, standing with him on his front porch.

He shouldn't pay attention to the way her expression, her slightly slumped shoulders, tugged at his heart.

But Jack was tired of doing exactly what he should. "Do you want to come in?" he asked. "Sammy would like it."

"I should go unpack boxes and get settled," she said, but then Sammy reached out a hand toward her hair, glowing like fire in the late-afternoon light.

Jack couldn't blame him. He'd like to know what that hair felt like, too.

"Aw, sweetie," she said, her face softening.

He opened the door, and she followed him inside.

Feeding Sammy, sharing a frozen pizza while he played on the floor, giving him a bath… All of it went as smoothly as if they'd been a long-established couple. "You read to him, right?" Arianna asked when Sammy started to rub his eyes with the backs of his hands.

"Every night." Sometimes Jack felt sheepish about that; Sammy was too young for stories, really, and had enough delays that it wasn't clear how much he followed. "It's just a nice way to spend time together. I try to keep the TV off until after he's in bed."

"Good." She knelt beside Jack's bookshelf, where board books mingled helter-skelter with Jack's own pre-ferred reading—military and legal thrillers. "How about a little *Hungry Caterpillar*, Sammy?"

Sammy watched her impassively.

"Brown Bear?" she asked, holding up another book.

Sammy patted his own head, rhythmically.

"He wants *From Head to Toe*," Jack said.

"Oh, with the gorilla!" She grabbed the book from the shelf and brought it over. She sat down on the other side of Sammy and handed the book to Jack.

"No, you read," he said.

"Because you like to act out the pictures?" she teased.

"You bet." He usually did, hoping the concepts would get through to Sammy. But today, he was just glad that the melancholy look was gone from Arianna's face, the tears from her eyes.

She opened to the first page and held up the book so both Sammy and Jack could see. "Look at the penguin, how it's bending its neck. Can you do like the penguin?"

Jack turned his neck.

Sammy watched.

"Good job!" she said to Jack, grinning at him.

She went on, reading slowly and expressively, through the animals and their various abilities: giraffe, buffalo, monkey, seal, with Jack doing the actions in response. He felt silly at first, but Arianna's smiles and occasional giggles made him comfortable.

"Look at the gorilla, guys. Can you thump your chest like a gorilla?"

"I can," Jack boasted and did it.

Sammy thumped his chest, too.

Arianna sucked in a breath. "He did it," she whispered. "He imitated you and he did what the book said."

Jack was hardly breathing, his heart too full of joy. At the same time, he was willing Arianna not to make a big fuss; Sammy hated that. "Good job, buddy," he said quietly when he could speak.

Arianna leaned over and planted a kiss on Sammy's head, and then read on.

It was the only response Sammy gave, but it was a first, and it was enough.

His heart was full as he picked Sammy up. "Time for bed, my man."

"I should go," Arianna said.

"You don't want to help me put him to bed?"

"I…I'd better not."

Sammy gave a great yawn.

"Don't leave," Jack ordered. He carried Sammy upstairs before she could answer, not even looking at her. Because what right did he have to ask her to stay?

He put Sammy down and patted his back for a few minutes, prayed over him as he did every night and added an extra prayer for guidance and wisdom for himself. He didn't have to specify what situation he needed guidance in. The Lord knew.

When he walked downstairs, he didn't know whether to hope she'd listened to him and stayed or ignored him and left. But she was there, looking out the window to the moonlit yard.

He walked up behind her. Seemingly of its own volition, his hand came up to rest on her shoulder. "Pretty night."

She nodded. And didn't shrug him away.

"Thanks for helping with Sammy tonight. He's never responded to that book before."

She turned her head a little, her dimple showing. "That was amazing."

"It made me very happy."

"Me, too."

In a circle of moonlit intimacy, sharing joy about his son, there didn't seem to be a lot of decisions to make. What to do seemed obvious.

He tugged at her shoulder until she turned around, then touched her chin.

She looked up, her eyes wide. "Jack—"

When she didn't finish what she was saying, he let his finger trace her full lips, light as you'd touch a newborn kitten. "I want to kiss you."

She drew in her breath, and he expected her to pull away.

Instead, she lifted her hand to cup his cheek.

"I need to shave," he said.

"It's okay."

He took that as a yes and kissed her.

Jack's lips moved gently on hers, but the kiss swept through Arianna like an electrical current. She sighed and pulled him closer.

He responded immediately, deepening the kiss, his fingers rising up to fork through her hair, then settling on the back of her head. And instantly, as if the mountain breeze had blown them away, her doubts and worries disappeared.

Being this close to Jack was all the warmth and love and caring she hadn't even known she was missing. It penetrated, too, that warmth: all the way through her, settling into her heart. It was as if something deep inside her sighed and said, *You're safe.*

His hand circled over her back in a gentle massage.

She breathed and let herself feel the emotions and kissed him back.

Until a jarring inner voice scolded through her romantic haze. *Chloe would really, really not like it if she knew what you were doing.*

And that thought stole away the safe, happy feeling. Because what *was* she doing, kissing the man who'd been Chloe's husband? The man from whom she was keeping a terrible secret?

It took every ounce of willpower to turn her head away, then her body, then to step outside the circle of his arms.

"Um, I..." She trailed off. There just weren't words, and if there were, she wasn't sure she could get them out past the thickness in her throat.

Jack looked a little dazed, as well.

She needed to leave. She couldn't look at his vulnerable face anymore, that warmth in his eyes. She needed to focus on her duty, what was best for Sammy.

But what *was* best for Sammy? Couldn't it be this?

No, it can't be this. The voice in her head sounded like her mother, but it could be Chloe's or the counselor at the church she'd attended—once—in the city where she'd gone as a single, pregnant mother-to-be. Maybe it was even Jack's voice. He'd admired how pure Chloe was.

Arianna, unlike her sister, had made bad decisions, and she had to pay. Had to pay for lying by omission, too; Jack would be furious if he knew the secret she was keeping.

With his special needs, Sammy didn't need the additional confusion of having his nanny turn out to be his mother. "I should go," she said. Her voice sounded odd, breathless. "That was… Look, Jack, I don't want to do that again."

It wasn't true. She *did* want to do it again. She wanted to feel his arms around her and his warm lips on hers, to see that intense, caring look—already fading now—in his eyes.

"I'm sorry," he said. "I didn't mean to overstep." He was looking at her a little puzzled now, as if to say, *but you seemed to like it.*

"I'll see you later."

"We should talk about it."

She looked away. "Not now."

"Okay, then. I'll watch you get home safely."

"No need for that." Because if he did, she might turn around and run right back into his arms.

Sammy, bless him, let out a cry before Arianna could fall apart. "Go, take care of him," she urged Jack. "I'll just run across the yard and be home."

"Then we'll talk tomorrow," he said firmly. He tucked a stray strand of her hair behind her ear, his hand lingering on her cheek.

His touch burned. "Okay, sure." She spun away and headed toward the door. She had to escape. She wanted so desperately to melt into Jack's arms, to savor his embrace. Her whole chest ached with the longing for it.

Tough. You can't have it.

After letting herself out, she marched across the lawn. She reached the driveway that led to Penny's house. *Keep going.*

She walked across the yard toward the outdoor stairs that led to her apartment.

Keep going.

She could do it. She could make it inside before she broke down.

"Arianna." The jarring sound of a male voice—*not* Jack's—startled her, and then the shadowy figure of a man came into view. She yelped out a scream and spun away from the intruder, her heart pounding fast.

"Arianna! Arianna, it's me, Nathan."

Oh. Her knees went weak, and she sank down onto the bottom step. "You scared me half to death."

"I'm sorry," he said, kneeling beside her. Wrinkles formed between his heavy eyebrows. "I just… You rushed away so fast, back at the store. Can we talk for a few minutes?"

No. She wanted to forget about Nathan and what had happened between them. Especially now, when her emotions were raw. "I'm very tired and I have to work tomorrow. Can't it wait?"

He bit his lip and shook his head back and forth. "I'm only in town for a few days, and this has been eating me alive."

She opened her mouth to refuse. But his face was tortured, and she'd once cared about him. "Okay," she said. "A quick talk. I guess I can do that."

"Thank you." He knelt on the pavement, shivering. He wore a short-sleeved polo shirt and khakis, not nearly warm enough for a mountain night.

"Come on in," she said with a sigh. "We can have a cup of tea and talk about whatever you want to talk about."

"Half an hour maximum," he promised. "And…despite the past, you can trust me."

"I know I can," she said, patting his arm as she walked past him, leading him up the steps.

From Sammy's bedroom, Jack watched Arianna lead Nathan Donegal up the steps to her place and slammed his fist against the wall beside the window.

He felt like a complete fool.

Here he had laid his heart out for her, exposed his feelings, and now she had a date with her ex-boyfriend?

Not that Jack's time with her had been a date, of course. She was his employee, his former sister-in-law. She didn't have any obligation to him. She had probably set something up with Nathan when she'd seen him in town today and had been eager to get over to her place to meet him. It was Jack who had mucked everything up by kissing her.

But she responded. She seemed to like it.

Well, he thought she had. He'd thought he had heard a little sigh. Had thought she'd kind of melted into him. And when they'd broken apart, he'd thought he had seen some kind of warm emotion in her eyes.

But he wasn't the best at understanding women, as Chloe had let him know often enough. The other thing Chloe had pinned on him was that he had always had a crush on Arianna. Jack didn't think that was true. He had loved his wife and had never allowed his thoughts to venture toward her sister. He knew right from wrong.

But maybe Chloe had seen something he hadn't even been aware of himself. Maybe he had more feelings than he realized, and now they had led him astray, led him into thinking Arianna liked him when she didn't.

Sammy stirred in his crib, and Jack turned away from the window and went over to tuck his blue-and-white-checked bear back into his arms. Sammy's face smoothed, and his breathing became regular again.

This was what was important. That Sammy had a good life, that he get the treatment he needed, that he have loving caregivers.

Arianna's nanny gig had never been intended to be permanent. It was just until the end of the summer.

And now that Jack knew the boundaries he needed to set, he'd do it.

He would stay strictly professional with Arianna. He wouldn't comment if she went out with Nathan. He wouldn't set up any more of these late evenings that created feelings he shouldn't be having, feelings that could only lead to unhappiness. At the end of the workday, he would wave goodbye and send her away without a personal element in it. His father would be proud. Chloe would be proud.

He drew in a couple of deep breaths and tried to congratulate himself on the rightness of his decision.

The fact that he himself felt empty, gutted even, shouldn't signify.

Arianna watched Nathan drain the last of his tea, his Adam's apple bulging.

"I can't believe Chloe told you about my pregnancy," she said. Although she kind of could. Chloe wasn't one to leave any loose ends if she could help it.

"She said you were going to place the baby for adoption, and she didn't want me to show up later and cause problems. I guess she didn't realize you hadn't told me at all."

"I should have." Arianna's heart twisted with regret and misery. She'd made so many mistakes. "It's no justification, but I was immature. Naive and so confused. And when I came to you to ask if you wanted to continue the relationship, you said—"

"I said I didn't. I know." He leaned forward, elbows propped on knees. "You suspected you were pregnant then, didn't you?"

"I knew it," she admitted.

"I wish you'd told me."

She shook her head. "I should have. I meant to, but you were so excited about your new research fellowship in Boulder. And you said you'd be working day and night."

"Yes, but it was my responsibility," he said. "If we made a baby together, I should have taken care of it." He splayed his hands in front of him and studied them.

Arianna's throat tightened. It was a gesture she'd seen Sammy make.

Nathan glanced up at her and then back down at his hands. "I only realized how wrong I was when my pastor spoke about how important fathers are, and how many don't take responsibility for their children. It hit me like a brick to the head that I was in that group, too."

"I suppose, though it wasn't on purpose. You can't be blamed for it."

"There's no way to find out more about the family who adopted our baby?"

Heat rose from her chest to her neck and spread to her cheeks. She prayed that the light was too dim for him to see how red her face was. "Like I said, it's a closed adoption," she said and hoped his steel-trap brain wouldn't close in on the fact that she hadn't answered his question.

"You can put a letter on file, and when he comes of age, if he wants to, he can contact you. But, Nathan…think about it, okay? You'll probably have a wife and kids by that time. You might not want to be in touch."

"So it's a boy." He rested his cheek on his interlocked hands, looking away from her.

"It's a boy."

He blew out a sigh and stood. "I'm sorry, Arianna. Sorry for pushing you into what we did together, and sorry for not standing by you."

She shook her head. "Don't apologize. We were equally at fault. I'm sorry I didn't insist on your hearing the whole truth."

They hugged, and she stood at the door and watched him go downstairs and out of her life. For now.

She sagged back against the door after she'd closed it behind him, too distraught even to think. "Lord, forgive me," she whispered.

It was the millionth time she'd prayed that, of course. But now there were new prayers to add. "Forgive Nathan and help him to find peace. And turn all of this messy situation to good. Amen."

She slid down the door to a sitting position, forehead on upraised knees. And there she sat for a long time in wordless prayer and meditation, desperately needing the peace that only God could give.

Chapter Nine

One awkward week later, Jack found himself at the office after everyone on his staff had gone home. He was catching up on paperwork, sure, but more than that, he was avoiding Arianna.

Every time he saw her, he thought about kissing her. Relived it, really—her warmth and tenderness and the way being close with her had filled a hole in his heart he hadn't even realized was there. His hands practically ached to pull her close to him again.

But there had always been reasons not to be with Arianna—Chloe's criticism and his parents' warnings—and those reasons hadn't gone away, not really. Yes, Chloe was gone. But for him to pick up with Arianna as much as proved that her suspicions had been right, that Jack hadn't really loved her, that he had been that neglectful, uncaring husband she had so often accused him of being.

And Chloe's critical glare, so vivid in his memory, would be mirrored on his father's face were he to get together with Arianna.

Even those things might have been surmountable, but

now he'd found out she had feelings for somebody else. Her relationship with Nathan must have been more serious than he'd thought, and from the looks of things, it was ongoing. Otherwise, why would she have taken Nathan up to her apartment?

It was true that he hadn't seen Nathan around in the week since the man had arrived in town. If Arianna were spending time with him, she was keeping it very quiet. So maybe Jack had overreacted. After all, Nathan lived up in Boulder and was a busy, well-known scientist. It would be tough for him to start, or restart, a relationship with a nanny-artist who lived in the southern part of the state.

Whenever he got to this part in his ruminations, a little spark of hope would come to life inside him. Guilt, though, due to Chloe and his father, quickly put out the flame.

So he was stressed. And he noticed that Sammy was fussier than usual, which could very well be because he was picking up on the tension between Jack and Arianna. That and the fact that Jack was working longer hours, so he wasn't spending as much time with his son as he should.

And if his state of mind was affecting Sammy, then Jack needed to do something about it. He didn't like asking for help, but he knew he had to overcome that, to swallow his pride, when Sammy was involved. So he closed up his office and walked two blocks down the street to his church, where his good friend Carson Blair was the pastor.

He walked through the cool, dark hallways. The light was still on in the church office, so he knocked.

"Come on in," came a deep but nasal voice.

Jack pushed the door open.

Hawk, honk. Carson was blowing his nose, and then he tossed the tissue into an overflowing wastebasket and looked up apologetically. "Hey, Jack," he said and coughed. "Glad to see you, but you might want to keep your distance. This cold is getting the best of me."

"I have a strong immune system," Jack said. "But I'm not stupid. I won't shake your hand." He studied his friend more closely. "Are you sure you should even be at work?"

"I canceled my appointments," Carson said. "But sermons don't write themselves. And Lily and the girls are visiting one of her old army friends, so I'm a bachelor this week. I may as well sneeze and cough here at the office as at home." He held up a hand. "And don't worry. Mrs. Greer will scrub everything down when she comes in in the morning."

"Oh, true." Jack had seen their church secretary disinfecting doorknobs and microphones, and once, she'd rushed up to the front of the church right in the middle of Carson's communion prayers to give him the hand sanitizer she'd forgotten to place with the bread and grape juice.

"What brings you here at this time of day?" Carson asked.

"I need to talk to you about something, and it seems like you could use a good meal. Can I buy you dinner? We'll go somewhere in town, close by."

"Sounds good to me," Carson said. "But don't you need to get home to Sammy?"

"Let me see if my nanny can stay a bit late."

"Your nanny, huh?" Carson cocked his head to the side and glanced questioningly at Jack. Then he turned back to his computer. "I'll just make a couple notes while you call her."

But Jack had no intention of calling Arianna; instead, he sent her a text.

Almost instantly, she texted back. No problem. No plans tonight.

Hmm, interesting. She didn't have plans. And she was making sure he knew it.

There was that tiny spark of hope again.

Half an hour later, they were at La Boca Feliz, and Senora Ramos, known to everyone as Delfina, was fussing over Carson. "*Sopa de tortilla* for you," she said. "Why are you not home in bed?"

"Lily and the kids are away," Carson croaked.

Delfina put her hands on her hips. "And you are not capable of opening a can of soup?" She turned to Jack. "And you could not help your friend?"

"I *am* helping him," Jack said. "I've brought him here for your healthy food."

Delfina smiled, her brown eyes twinkling. "This is the good answer," she said and clapped her hands as she turned toward the kitchen. "Emilio, *dos sopas de tortillas, por favor. El pastor está enfermo.*"

They both watched as she disappeared into the kitchen. Around them, silverware clinked and customers talked and laughed.

"So, what's going on with you?" Carson asked.

In the course of helping Carson, Jack had forgotten about his own problems for a few minutes, and he didn't really want to reengage with them. He lifted his hands, palms up. "No big deal. Nothing you need to worry about."

"I always worry about my flock," Carson said. "It's in the job description."

Delfina bustled back toward them, carrying a tray with two brimming bowls of soup. She set one before each of them. "Eat, both of you. More food is coming."

Jack lifted an eyebrow. "Did we order more?"

"You didn't have to," Delfina retorted. "I placed the order myself, because I know what's good for a cold. And—" she pointed at Jack "—don't tell me you don't have a cold, because spending time with him, you will."

"I hope not," Carson said after she'd left them for another table. "I'd hate to be the reason you and Sammy get sick."

Jack waved a hand to dismiss Carson's worry. "We have so many TSS folks in and out of the house, plus Arianna's got him in some baby lap-sit program at the library. I'm sure he's been exposed to whatever germs you're carrying." He started spooning up soup, hot and spicy and delicious.

"Good." Carson ate for a few minutes and then put down his spoon. "I'd like to hear about whatever's worrying you."

Jack could tell from the determined look in Carson's eyes that the man wasn't going to give up. They were the same age, but Carson was wise, far wiser than Jack, especially in matters of the spirit and the heart. "I'm just struggling some," he admitted. When Carson nodded encouragingly, he went on. "There's something Chloe thought about me that I'm having a hard time shaking."

Carson frowned. "Was it true, what she thought?"

"No. At least, I don't think so."

"It's no fun to be harshly judged," Carson said. "Believe

me, I've been there. And that judgmental voice doesn't have to be true to nag at you."

"Makes me question myself," Jack admitted. Because if Chloe, and his mom, and his dad all believed that Jack had a crush on Arianna, was it possible that he did and didn't know it?

As if he were reading Jack's mind, Carson pointed his soupspoon at Jack and spoke again. "How does it all connect with what you were told as a child? How you were raised?"

Jack laughed, even though he didn't find the question funny. "'Harshly judged' could have been in my parents' marriage vows, they made such a practice of it. Toward me, toward each other and toward themselves."

"So Chloe came along and fitted right in with your concept of love," Carson said.

His words echoed in Jack's ears as Delfina brought them plates of steaming enchiladas and rice and beans, explained that they were extra spicy and that was good for a cold, and admonished them to eat every bite.

As Jack dug in, he thought about what Carson had said. Was that his concept of love: Harsh judgment? Was that why he and Chloe had hit it off?

They ate until they had to pause to wipe the sweat from their foreheads. "She wasn't kidding about spicy," Jack said, gulping water.

"I think I'm sweating out my germs. I sure don't feel congested anymore." He studied Carson. "Why are these questions about Chloe and your past coming up now? Because of Arianna?"

Jack blew out a breath. "There's no keeping anything from you, is there? Is it obvious?"

Carson shook his head. "Not obvious. The two of

you are very circumspect and professional around each other. But I know you pretty well. I'm seeing something different in the way you confront the world, something that seems like it might come from… I don't know. Interest? Love?"

Jack nearly choked on a mouthful of beans. He waved his hand. "Nothing close to love. Interest, maybe. But that's where the past is bogging me down." He didn't want to disrespect Chloe's memory by telling Jack about her jealousy issues. "I'm just not sure whether it's right to let Chloe go and get back in the game again. Or when that might be okay."

"It's tough." Carson looked unseeingly across the crowded restaurant, and Jack remembered the trouble Carson had had accepting the loss of his first wife and moving on, until Lily had come along and rocked the pastor's world.

But Carson *had* accepted his loss and moved on, and no one had judged him for it.

"I'm going to email you a list of Scripture verses about guilt, and how to get free of it," Carson said. "Once you've grieved and healed from your past hurts and losses, you have to make your own decisions, independent of what others might think. I don't know about your wife, but my first wife had mental health issues that colored the way she looked at everything. It took some work for me to realize that wasn't my fault. Work and prayer." He pushed his plate away. "I'll also be praying for you to discern the right next step," he said.

"Thanks." Jack was grateful that Carson wasn't the type to hold his hand and pray publicly.

There wasn't an opportunity anyway, because old Tecumseh Smith stopped by the table to tell Jack about the digestive difficulties his mule was having, in colorful detail. Jack kept eating and nodding and offering advice, until he noticed that Carson was looking a little green and brought the conversation to an end.

"Sorry," he said to Carson after Tecumseh walked away. "Forgot that not everyone likes to discuss mule intestines while they eat."

"You did not eat enough!" Delfina approached the table and frowned at Carson's half-full plate.

"Can you wrap it up for me, senora?" Carson asked. "I'll have it for lunch tomorrow. I'm feeling better already."

"I will box it up with another carton of soup," she said and whisked away their plates. Jack insisted on paying— it was the least he could do—and they walked the short distance back to their vehicles in the cool evening twilight. "Just remember," Carson said as they were about to part ways. "You're not doomed to repeat the past. God can make all things new, and that includes you. You're a new creation, and anything is possible with Him."

"I hope you're right."

"I *am* right. It's all in the Bible." Carson held up an arm as a barrier, avoiding Jack's handshake. "I don't want to get you sick. Thanks for the dinner, man."

"Thank *you*," Jack said and walked back to his truck with more of a spring in his step than he'd had in days.

He wasn't going to delude himself that one conversation with Carson had resolved all his issues, but it had helped. He no longer dreaded seeing Arianna back at the ranch. Truth to tell, he was looking forward to it.

"So, did you have a good time with Branson?" Arianna asked Penny. The older woman had come over shortly after Jack had texted her to ask her to stay late. Now she was trying to avoid Penny's perceptive questions about what was going on between her and Jack.

They were sitting in Jack's kitchen, watching the sun set over the Sangre de Cristos. Sammy had been exhausted from a trip to the Esperanza Springs library's baby lap sit followed by a TSS appointment, so Arianna had put him to bed half an hour early.

"Branson's a very nice man," Penny said. "He brought flowers and a side dish—this couscous salad," she added, pointing to the dish she'd brought, "that he'd made himself."

"Which is really good," Arianna said, taking another bite of it. "I mean, how many guys would use fresh dill and oregano?"

"How many men even know what couscous is?" Penny asked, chuckling. "I had to sneak off to the bathroom and look it up on my phone so I didn't seem like too much of a country bumpkin."

Arianna laughed. "That's not the image I have of you, believe me. And that's also not what I asked. I asked if you had a good time." This was good. Looked like she'd be able to grill Penny for a little while here, help her figure out what was obvious to Arianna—that she preferred Willie to the banker—and, in the process, keep her own romantic issues off the table.

"I don't know. It's just not...comfortable, you know? I feel like he's trying to prove himself to me."

"As he should. You undersell yourself. You're a very attractive, smart, successful woman."

Penny snorted. "Who's barely gotten the ranch out of the red, and whose husband left her for the secretary.

Not even his secretary, *my* secretary. But I don't want to talk about me."

"Let's talk about these kebabs, then. They're so tender. And not even fattening."

"Why you worry so much about your figure, I'll never understand." Penny sipped her iced tea. "Believe me, there will come a day when you'll look back on that smooth, perfect skin and those hourglass curves and wish you had them back."

"Doubtful," Arianna said. And then their conversation moved to the art therapy group Arianna was doing at the ranch, and how well the veterans were responding, and whether it was time to start a second group.

"Jack's keeping pretty late hours," Penny said finally, glancing up at the clock.

Arianna clapped a hand to her mouth. "Oh no, he'll be home any minute, and the place is a mess." She stood and started clearing plates. "Please stay, Penny, if you don't mind my doing a little cleaning while we talk." She hurried a load of dishes to the sink and then turned back for more.

Penny was looking at her, head cocked to one side. "Are you always this paranoid about the state of the house?"

"Oh, well, my mom was really a clean freak. So is Jack. And I'm more the slob type."

Penny stood and carried the serving dishes to the counter. "I look around this place—and your place—and I don't see a slob. I see someone who's creative and who's been taking care of a baby all day."

"Yes, but Sammy went to bed an hour ago." She should have cleaned up the living room right away rather than collapsing on the couch and reading a novel.

"And shortly after he went down, you got unexpected company," Penny said, pointing at her own chest. "Whom you greeted very hospitably, I might add."

Arianna loaded plates and silverware into Jack's state-of-the-art dishwasher. "You're sure of a good welcome when you come bearing food."

"I was glad for someone to share it with. Glad for some girl time." Penny found a sponge and started wiping down Sammy's high chair, and Arianna didn't have the heart to tell her that she was using the counter sponge, not the Sammy sponge. Or did she have that wrong? Maybe the blue one was for Sammy.

"Anyway," she said, "Jack's pretty orderly, and he's paying me well, so I'm trying to be neater than I would be on my own."

"This room looks fine," Penny said, returning the possibly incorrect sponge to the dish by the sink. "Come on, let's tackle the living room, and you can tell me about your mom."

They'd gotten the place into a semblance of order, and Penny was laughing about Arianna's stories of competing with her sister for neatness awards their mother had set up, when Arianna heard the rumble of Jack's truck.

Her stomach tightened.

Things had been so uncomfortable between them since that wonderful, terrible kiss. Jack had backed way off, obviously avoiding her. What was up with that? Was he one of the many men who preferred the chase to the conquest?

But it was you who told him you didn't want to do it anymore, she reminded herself.

And for very good reason. How could she justify

keeping secret the fact that she was Sammy's mother if her relationship with Jack deepened?

And yet how could she justify telling Jack something she'd promised never to tell, and something that would undoubtedly sully his view not only of her, but of Chloe?

The door opened and Jack came in, and all of a sudden the house seemed the way it should again.

Well, except for the baby toys that still littered one end of the living room.

"Hey, Penny," he said as he stowed his briefcase and picked up the mail. "How's it going?"

"*I'm* going," the older woman answered. "Arianna and I were having a nice visit, but I've got an early morning tomorrow." She opened the door, then tossed over her shoulder, "Don't give her too hard of a time about the state of the house. It's tough to keep it looking like a showpiece when you're taking care of a baby."

As the door closed behind her, Jack stared at Arianna. "You've been keeping the place extra neat for me," he said.

"I've been trying," she admitted. "Fallen down on the job today a little."

He put down the mail and grabbed a can of soda from the kitchen while she finished straightening the living room. She was just about to gather her things when he came back into the front room, sat down and patted the couch beside him. "Penny's right," he said. "It's hard with a baby. And everything looks just fine. Can we talk?"

Arianna's heart stuttered. He was going to fire her.

She was going to lose the chance to care for her son. Lose the chance to be near Jack. And suddenly, her on-the-road life as an art therapist, a perfectly good and adequate life, didn't even seem palatable.

Tears pushed at the backs of her eyes and she drew in deep breaths, trying to keep them from falling. Miserably, she approached the couch and sat down beside him.

"Look, Arianna," he said, his expression gentle and kind, which meant disaster, of course. "It's been…awkward between us."

She nodded, both because it was true and because she couldn't speak.

"That kiss was…premature." He kept his eyes on hers. "I'm sorry for that. I've been happy—very happy—with your work with Sammy. And…" He hesitated, his face coloring a little. "And I like being around you," he added finally. "Do you think we could try to go back to that, to the way we were before?"

Her insides were dancing so fast that she could barely find the wherewithal to nod.

He'd said "premature." Not a mistake, not wrong, just premature.

Did that mean he was good with it happening? Even that he wanted it to happen again?

At any rate, he hadn't fired her, and that meant she could continue working with Jack and with her son. "I'd like that," she managed to choke out through a throat tight with gratitude.

But as she gathered her things, an uneasy feeling penetrated her happiness. She hadn't told Jack about Sammy's heritage, and that fact stood in the way of them ever getting closer.

Tell him.

It wasn't an audible voice, there in the moonlight as she walked across the lawn to her place, Jack watching from the porch. It was just a feeling in her heart, but she knew the author of that feeling, because it was the same message she'd gotten in prayer before.

It was true, probably; she should tell him. But she was afraid. Afraid of hurting this wonderful, tentative, fragile accord between them.

Afraid of being barred from caring for her son.

Chapter Ten

"Are you ready, Sammy? Ready to take the dog to Miss Arianna?" Jack didn't have to strain to put excitement in his voice, something the TSS had recommended.

Sammy's face remained impassive, but he toddled over to the door, which, as Arianna always pointed out, was a clear form of communication.

Jack scooped up the eight-week-old puppy he'd just examined and wrapped it in a towel, and they headed over to Arianna's place.

It was a beautiful Sunday afternoon. From the mountains, a warm breeze blew the scent of pine, rich and resinous. A Steller's jay squawked from a nearby aspen tree, scolding them, maybe scolding Jack for the eager anticipation he was feeling.

He and Arianna had a new, fragile accord, and he treasured it. After the awkwardness of that week after they kissed, Jack was being cautious not to reveal the attraction he felt for his redheaded nanny.

That attraction had caused them problems before. He didn't want to risk their friendship by acting on it again.

Then what are you going to do with the attraction?

Because he wasn't going to stop feeling it, that much was clear. So was he just going to shove it aside and continue treating Arianna as a friend? That seemed like it might be really hard to do. But on the other hand, if he made another move to get closer to Arianna, he might scare her away entirely.

When he'd hired her, it had been for a temporary position, just for the summer. She'd planned to seek work elsewhere if she couldn't find a permanent art therapy job here. But now the thought of her leaving stabbed at his heart.

He looked up at the clear blue sky. *Father, You're going to have to take over, because I don't know what to do, and I keep messing this up.*

He helped Sammy climb the first couple of stairs and then knelt and scooped him up to carry him the rest of the way to Arianna's second-floor apartment. Sammy's walking was improving, but stairs were a challenge still, of course.

At the top, arms full of puppy and boy, he tapped on the door. "Dog delivery," he called through the screen.

From inside Arianna's apartment, a loud squeal erupted and then Arianna ran through her small kitchen to the door, talking a mile a minute. "Did you bring me my puppy? I'm so excited! I can't believe I get to have him!" She opened the door and held out her hands, and Jack carefully shifted the puppy into her arms before putting Sammy down.

"He is so precious! I can't believe how tiny he is. And how wiggly!" She knelt so she could be at the same level as Sammy. Of course. She was always conscious of that, always trying to include him, to teach him new things.

"Look how cute he is, Sammy," she said. "Oh, Jack, I love him already."

Jack could have stood there and watched her for an hour as she cuddled the puppy and showed it to Sammy and put it down on the floor to let it walk and laughed at its clumsiness.

Her feet were bare, her toenails painted bright pink. He swallowed, then cleared his throat. "Do you have everything you need? You got bowls and food and a bed?"

Great, he sounded like a scold.

But rather than being annoyed, Arianna bobbed her head up and down and rose to her feet, graceful, the puppy in her arms. "Come see. You can tell me if I got the right stuff."

So Jack took Sammy's hand, and they followed her through the little apartment. She showed him the food and water bowls, simple and basic, just what Jack would have purchased himself. "And I got the puppy chow you recommended. And a few treats." She smiled a bit guiltily and showed him four different kinds of dog biscuits. "Are these okay for him to eat?"

Jack had to laugh at her. "They're fine. It's okay to indulge a puppy. Everyone does."

In the living room, more of that indulgence was on display. In addition to a small crate, she had gotten the little dog a warm fleece bed and at least eight different toys.

"I know, I know, I went overboard," she said. "They had a sale. That's my excuse." She put the dog down, and they all knelt around it. The puppy pounced on a banana-shaped toy, then jumped back when the toy squeaked.

Jack and Arianna laughed, and then Sammy let out a sound that could or could not have been a laugh, and

Jack's eyes met Arianna's. Her smile was brilliant. And Jack could tell his own face held a similar expression.

"You know," she said, "if it turns out that Buster would be a good dog for Sammy to have, I'll give him to you."

"No, he's yours," Jack protested.

"Sammy is the priority," she said firmly. "If I'm just the puppy raiser for his service dog, I'm okay with that."

Her words sent a wave of happiness through Jack. One, because of the idea of Sammy having a service dog. That just might make a big difference for him. And two, he was impressed by Arianna's generosity and willingness to sacrifice.

Strange, on paper Chloe had been the upright, perfectly behaved, rule-following sister. Women's committee at church, Sunday school teacher, always tastefully dressed, a great cook and housekeeper.

According to Chloe, Arianna was the one who had gotten in all kinds of trouble as a kid. She'd struggled in school and wrecked her car and gotten into fights with her parents.

But as adults, and maybe this was because of Arianna's childhood difficulties, Arianna was the more generous and compassionate one. It seemed like Chloe had gotten more and more rigid. And living with her, Jack knew better than anyone the anxiety and tension that had hovered just beneath her perfect facade. It had gotten to the point that it made her miserable, and Jack had begged her to seek counseling. But she had refused, because that would have destroyed her carefully crafted self-image.

After a few more minutes, Sammy turned away, his signal that he had had enough. Arianna read it as quickly as Jack did, and she found a board book and helped

Sammy sit down in a quiet corner on his blanket. There, he turned the pages methodically, tapping his foot on the floor in a complicated rhythm.

The puppy seemed to be overwhelmed at the same moment. He walked and climbed and tumbled his way into the fleece bed, flopped down on his side and fell instantly asleep.

So now it was just Jack and Arianna, her on the couch and him in the armchair catty-corner, because he wasn't going to push himself on her by sitting too close on the couch. But that good resolution was negated by the question he couldn't help asking. "Have you seen Nathan lately?"

She looked at him, surprise evident in her expression. "No, I haven't. I think he's gone back to the university."

"Are you upset about that?"

Now she really looked puzzled. "No, I'm not. Why would I be?" Color climbed into her cheeks.

Jack observed her narrowly even as he shrugged and lifted his hands, palms up. "No particular reason."

She didn't *seem* upset about Nathan being gone, and that made his heart beat a little faster. Did that mean she would be open to exploring a deeper connection with Jack?

But on the other hand, he was pretty sure there was something about Nathan that she wasn't telling him.

Restless now, he stood and paced around the little living room. "You have it set up so nice." With the colorful pillows and throws, the rattan shades at the windows and the hanging plants, the place already looked artsy and fun, just like Arianna herself.

He glanced at the photos on the mantel and paused at a picture of Chloe and Arianna, probably taken when they were teenagers. They both had their heads thrown back, laughing. Jack swallowed. "This is a good shot," he said, nodding sideways at the picture.

Arianna came to stand beside him. "I love it," she said. "There weren't that many times when we laughed together, but I treasure the few happy moments we had."

"What was it that put you two so much at odds?" Jack really wanted to know. He felt like it would solve some of the mystery of Chloe, help him resolve the past.

She picked up the photo and then put it down again, sighing. "Mostly, it was our mom. I guess she was trying to help us both excel by pitting us against each other. But I don't think it really worked. Sisterhood shouldn't be a competition."

"Chloe was jealous of you, you know." As soon as the words were out of his mouth, Jack regretted them. He didn't want to betray Chloe by letting Arianna know her deeper feelings.

But to his surprise, Arianna just nodded. "We were jealous of each other," she said. "I always wanted to be perfectly groomed and well organized the way that she was. She was in every club and organization. She got straight As. She was the perfect one."

Jack knew what she meant, but he couldn't let that analysis go. "She didn't feel perfect. Not inside herself."

"I know." She sighed. "In some ways, it was easier to be me than it was to be her. She came close to meeting Mom's standards, and that motivated her to try harder and harder all the time. I was so far below them that I just did my own thing."

"She thought I was attracted to you."

Arianna sucked in a breath. "What?"

He nodded. *May as well go through with this now.*

"She got kind of obsessed with the idea that I wanted to be with you. That's why she didn't want you to come to our house very often. When you did, it always left her in a terrible funk."

Color had risen in Arianna's cheeks. "Wow, I didn't know that," she said. She glanced up at his face and then looked away just as quickly.

He'd better push it to the end now. "She was wrong," he said. "I never wanted to be with another woman while I was with Chloe. Our marriage wasn't perfect, but I loved her, and I was loyal to her. It's important to me that you know that."

"I never would have doubted it, Jack," she said quietly.

"It's a little confusing to me," he said, "because now I *do* feel attracted to you."

Again she flashed a glance at him and then looked away, biting her lip.

"But I guess you know that."

She nodded almost imperceptibly, not looking up at him.

"Look, Arianna, I don't know where it might lead, but I would like to know you better in a social way, not just this employer-employee way." He drew in a breath. Asking for a date didn't get any easier than it had been when he was a teenager. He cleared his throat. "Would you like to go to the Redemption Ranch fund-raising gala with me?"

Arianna stared at Jack, wondering if her ears had deceived her. "Did you just ask me out?"

"I did." Jack looked at her for a moment and then stepped away, pacing over to the window and back again. "But, Arianna, I hope you know you can say no without causing any kind of a problem in our employer-employee relationship."

Her thoughts raced faster than she could process. On one side of her mind, an excited girl jumped up and down and clasped her hands together and squealed, *He asked me out! He asked me out!*

Another side of her, the more rational side, tried to project out into the future. He'd asked her out. If she went, and if they had fun, maybe he would ask her out again. And again.

At what point would it be right for her to say, "Hey, Jack, you know your son Sammy? Well, he's my biological child"?

Never. It would never be right for her to say that. Especially when she had promised her sister she wouldn't. And her sister wasn't around for her to renegotiate their agreement.

But if she turned down his invitation, which was what all logic suggested, her heart would break.

"I don't have a formal dress" was what she ended up saying.

"That's no problem," he said promptly. "I still have some of Chloe's dresses in storage. I can pull them out for you, and you can try them on while Sammy is napping one day."

Did he have no concept of sizes? Did he not remember that Chloe had been a stick while Arianna was much more, um, full figured?

Did he not realize that wearing one of Chloe's dresses would feel just plain weird?

Maybe he did have a concept of size, because he said, "Chloe fluctuated in size quite a bit during our marriage, and I think there are formal dresses in every size she ever wore. So it would be like shopping. You could take your pick."

"Jack…I'm sure they wouldn't fit," she said. "But… maybe I could shop for a dress."

"Then you will go to the gala with me?" Jack's intense gaze left no doubt that he really wanted her to.

And it was that, that strong desire for her company, the sweet balm of it soothing her heart, that convinced her. "Yes, I'll go."

Go to her own doom, most likely.

The next day, Arianna ended up leaving the puppy with Jack and taking Sammy out shopping. "Best to get him out of here in the hopes he doesn't catch whatever I've got," Jack croaked. He was staying home from work because of the monster cold he'd contracted. "Me and Buster will catch up on our rest."

Willie's ancient pickup truck chugged up to the driveway area between Jack's house and Penny's, and Arianna took Sammy's hand. "We'll be a couple of hours, max," she said to Jack. "Penny's shopping for a dress, too, but I have a feeling she's not a shop-all-day kind of person."

"I'm not sure why Willie is taking you," Jack said. "One or both of you could have driven."

"True, but—" Arianna smiled "—if I had to guess why he made the offer, I'd say he wants to spend the time around Penny."

"You're probably right, but he must be *really* motivated to put up with clothes shopping."

"That's a bad attitude," she said with mock sternness. "I'll try to train Sammy differently. Now, you rest up and don't worry. Sammy's in good hands."

"I know that," he said, and his gaze on her was warm.

His obvious approval melted something that had long been frozen inside her. What would it be like to live in the warmth of that approval?

Flustered, she gathered Sammy and his bag and her purse and made her way out to Willie's truck. Penny helped her get the car seat from Jack's vehicle and they strapped Sammy in, and then the two women climbed into the front seat beside Willie.

"You're a better man than I am," Jack called out to Willie. "Guess you're *really* missing Long John."

"Long John ain't near as pretty as these two ladies," Willie said and gave Jack a wave as he pulled the truck out of the driveway.

Thirty minutes later, they were walking in the door of a funky little shop with a wild, psychedelic sign proclaiming they were entering Suzie's Gently Used Emporium.

The tiny shop was lined with clothing, with racks encircling the first floor and a narrow balcony above entirely lined with more clothes. Shoes and purses stood on display tables in the center of the store, along with colorful scarves and jewelry.

"If we can't find dresses here, they're not to be found. And Suzie's prices are very reasonable." Penny was already flipping through the nearest rack.

In Arianna's arms, Sammy stared, wide-eyed.

Having parked the truck, Willie came in and lifted Sammy out of her arms. "You shop. Sammy and I will walk around outside a little bit. It's a nice day."

As soon the door had closed behind them, Penny glanced over at Arianna. "In case you couldn't tell, he's mad at me," she said.

"Why?" Arianna had noticed the tension in the truck on the way down.

"Because just before we picked you and Sammy up, I told him I'm going to the fund-raiser with Branson Howe," she said. "He asked me first—what can I say?"

"Ouch." Arianna looked off in the direction Willie had gone, feeling sorry for him. "Which one do you like better?"

Penny lifted her hands, palms up. "I don't trust my feelings," she said. "They're what got me in trouble before." She pulled out a purple dress, frowned at it and put it back. "I've tried taking it to God, but so far, He's been quiet."

Arianna found a rack labeled with her size and started looking at dresses, too. "Do you sometimes hear from Him? God, I mean."

Penny looked at her quickly. "Yeah. I do. Do you?"

Arianna shook her head. "Not so far. I wish I would." And then she realized that wasn't quite true. She had heard from God. God had told her to tell Jack the truth.

She hadn't done it. Was that why God had gotten quiet on her?

A woman carrying a tablet and an armful of blouses came bustling out from the back. "Hi, Penny," she said. "Anything I can help you with?" She looked inquiringly at Arianna. "I don't think I know you. I'm Suzie, and I own this place. It's a bit of a jumble, but I can help you find what you need."

"Arianna Shrader. I'm helping out up at Redemption Ranch."

"We're both looking for dresses for a fund-raiser," Penny said. "Not exactly formal, but fancy."

"Cocktail length?"

Penny nodded. "Although there won't be any cocktails involved. It's a Redemption Ranch fund-raiser, and too many of our veterans struggle with alcohol."

"Right." Suzie climbed the steep stairs to the second level and made her way along that narrow walkway until she found what she was looking for. "Ready? Catch," she said from above and dropped a dress on Penny. Next, she walked a little farther along and pulled two dresses off hangers. "And these are for you, young lady," she said. "Beautiful with your red hair. Fitting room is in the corner, behind the cash register."

She and Penny took turns trying on the dresses. Penny came out in her elegant burnt-orange sheath just as Willie came back into the shop with Sammy. The older man stopped and stared. "You look so beautiful," he said with a catch in his voice.

The adoration in his eyes made Arianna decide right then: she was officially on Team Willie.

Judging from the way Penny colored up, Arianna thought she might be leaning in that direction, as well. How the older woman would work that out when she was slated to go to the fund-raiser with Branson, Arianna couldn't imagine.

After Penny had changed back into regular clothes, Arianna went in. She pulled on the turquoise dress and smoothed it down.

"Come out and show us," Penny called.

She did, and they oohed and aahed, but Suzie frowned. "Try the other one," she said.

"The other one is lime green," she protested. "I love the color, but I'm afraid it'll make me look fat. Don't you have anything in black?"

"I do," Suzie said, "and you'd look sophisticated in black, but try the green one first. Humor me."

Arianna put it on and smoothed it over her hips. It clung, maybe a little too much, but flared out into a wide ruffle at her knees. The bodice fitted perfectly, with a modest keyhole neckline and cap sleeves.

She loved it.

Hesitantly, she came out of the fitting room, and all three of the others exclaimed and nodded enthusiastically. Even Sammy offered the half smile that was becoming his trademark.

"It's so *you*," Penny said. "Creative and fun and lively. You have to get it."

"Not many of my customers could carry off that color," Suzie said. "So I'm going to give it to you at half price."

Arianna sucked in a breath. "You'd do that?"

"I would, as long as you promise to have a good time in it."

"I will," Arianna said. "God willing."

Only, if God willed her to have a good time, a wonderful time, on a fancy date with Jack…then what might He will for her to do next?

Jack was brooding, and he wasn't a brooder.

Oh, he was thrilled that Arianna had agreed to go out with him. But almost immediately, the worrier in him had kicked into action.

His father would undoubtedly hear about the fundraiser, most likely be there. And he wouldn't approve of Jack taking Arianna.

He'd admitted the truth to Arianna, that Chloe had been jealous, and she hadn't found it upsetting. Maybe because she and Chloe already had their issues. So that was the biggest hurdle.

His father's disapproval was a constant in Jack's life, but his worry was that his father would say something rude to Arianna.

If this was going to be the reality going forward—that he and Arianna were exploring a relationship—and he fervently hoped it would be, then he needed to confront his father.

His opportunity came unexpectedly quickly, when his father dropped by the ranch to give Jack some of his old toys that Sammy might be able to use. They even had a good time pulling the old rocking horse and blocks from Dad's trunk and reminiscing about Jack's childhood, though Jack made sure his father kept a good distance, not wanting to infect him with his cold.

"Dad," he said, "there's something I'd like to discuss with you."

"What's that?" Dad put down the plastic push mower he'd been wiping off.

Jack cleared his throat. "I'm taking Arianna to the Redemption Ranch gala."

"What? Do you know how that will look? People will think you're dating!"

Here goes nothing. "I hope we *will* date. I care about her, and I'd like to see where things go between us."

His father went back to wiping off the push mower, his movements jerky. "Then it's true, what Chloe always said."

Jack shook his head. "No. I was loyal to Chloe. I never thought about Arianna as anything other than a sister when Chloe was alive."

"Humph." Dad looked over at him, a glare from beneath

heavy eyebrows. "Your mother always thought there were problems in your marriage. I didn't."

"There were some problems." And Jack didn't want to go into them. "Doesn't every marriage have some problems?"

Dad lifted his chin. "Your mother and I had forty-five years of happiness."

"Really?" All too well Jack remembered the days of silence, the tight-lipped dinners, the icily polite interactions between his parents. But he certainly wasn't going to bring that up now. "I'm happy it was that way for you, Dad. Chloe and I had a lot of happy times, too." Before her anxieties had driven her to thoughts that had made her miserable. Again, like always, he wished he'd known better how to help his wife. He'd grieved double for her because he hadn't had time to do everything he'd meant to do to help her.

"I don't like it, son. You're making a mistake."

"I'm sorry you feel that way. I wanted you to know."

He was walking his father to the car when, unexpectedly, Willie's truck chugged up and parked beside Dad's Oldsmobile. The contrast was almost comical.

But Jack's tension rose. Would Dad say something awful to Arianna? Not everyone realized how sensitive she was beneath her fun-loving exterior.

Arianna jumped out, waved to his father and reached to extract Sammy from his car seat.

Penny climbed out. "You should see Arianna's dress," she said to Jack. "She's going to be the belle of the ball, and to think, she got the dress half-price from a thrift shop!"

Jack frowned. If Arianna were still so short on money that she couldn't afford a new dress, then why hadn't she taken him up on his offer of Chloe's dresses? They were all fashionable, some of them with designer labels.

His father was staring at Penny and Arianna. "Thrift shop? You're clothes shopping at a thrift shop?"

Penny smiled at him. "Hi, Mr. DeMoise. Suzie's Gently Used is one of Esperanza Springs' most successful businesses. Recycling at its best. I got my dress there, too."

Jack cleared his throat. "Actually, Dad, Mom sold a number of her dresses to Suzie's. As did Chloe."

"Selling clothes to those less fortunate is one thing. Buying them there is another," Dad said.

Arianna was standing against the car, a bag clutched in her hand. "Did Chloe, um, donate a lot of dresses to Suzie's?"

"She sold them on consignment, and yes." Jack could tell she felt uneasy from the look in her eyes. "Why?"

Slowly, Arianna opened her bag, pulled out a lime-green dress and held it up to herself. "There's no way this was one of Chloe's. Right?"

Jack stared at the dress he and Chloe had argued about. He'd bought it for her as a surprise, early in their marriage, and she'd hated it. Too loud. Too unusual. And why did he even think she could wear a size twelve? She'd been size eight, mostly, for years!

What were the odds Arianna would have come home with Chloe's dress? He cleared his throat. "Actually, that *was* one of hers. She never wore it," he added hastily. "She decided it wasn't her style."

The words hung in the air as everyone processed the awkwardness of the situation.

"I should say not," Dad bluffed. "A little exotic for Chloe."

Maybe I wished she were a little more exotic. The very thought made Jack's face burn. But he forced himself to think back. He'd thought she would like the dress. She liked green, and he'd known the style would suit her figure.

Remembering Chloe's reaction to the dress made Jack tense up. Would Arianna be as emotional as her sister had been, although for different reasons? Would she freak out, get upset, cry? She had every right to do so.

"Well," she said, with cheer in her voice that was only partially forced, "we do have the same coloring. I'd be honored to wear a dress Chloe picked out. She had really great taste."

Dad opened his mouth, and for a horrible moment, Jack thought he was going to make a quip about taste in men.

Willie came to the rescue, slapping Dad on the back. "That young gal sure is pretty, but you ought to see our Miss Penny in her new dress. It's the color of a sunset and fits her to a T. Brings out those amber eyes of hers."

"Oh, now, Willie," Penny said, and then Dad said he had to leave, and Penny and Willie went off toward her place.

Arianna swept up Sammy in her arms. "You," she said, pointing a finger at Jack, "need to get back to bed. You look terrible. And Sammy needs you to be healthy."

"I'm sorry about all that," he said, not moving toward the house, but pointing at the bag into which she'd stuffed the green dress. "I had no idea you were going to shop at Suzie's, and even if I'd known, I don't think I'd have imagined that you would light on a dress of Chloe's."

"I didn't light on it, exactly," she said, her voice thoughtful. "Miss Suzie went and picked it out especially for me. I didn't even think it would look good on me, but it was perfect. Was she friends with Chloe?"

"Let's just say they did business together. Chloe bought a lot of clothes and changed sizes a lot, so she tried to recoup some of her money there."

Arianna nodded. "It's just a little weird that the store owner would choose that particular dress for me to try on. I'm trying to remember whether Penny introduced me by name, whether she might have known my connection to Chloe."

"Arianna," he said, "anyone who looked at you would know you're connected to Chloe. You guys look so similar."

"Really?" Arianna cocked her head to one side. "I never thought so. And Mom always said…" She trailed off and looked away. "We should get you and Sammy both inside and into bed."

"What did your mom always say?"

Arianna frowned. "She said that Chloe was the beauty *and* the brains," she said slowly, "and that I was the ditz."

He blew out a breath and shook his head. Amazing what some people considered good parenting.

"If the shoe fits," Arianna said. "Believe me, Jack, 'ditz' is one of the nicer names she called me. I was always failing to live up to her expectations. I was a real loser in high school."

He wanted to put his arms around her so badly that his whole body ached with it, but he didn't. It would be inappropriate, and besides, he didn't want to pass along his germs. "You're not a loser in my book," he settled for saying.

Now wasn't the time to pull her closer. But maybe, just maybe, the fund-raiser would be.

Chapter Eleven

As they pulled into the parking lot of the upscale Mission Hotel for the fund-raiser, Arianna struggled with herself.

She couldn't deny it: she was completely thrilled to be on a date with Jack. He'd insisted on coming to her door, had brought her flowers, had moved quickly ahead to open the passenger door for her. He'd joked and chatted with her on the way down to Esperanza Springs, making her feel comfortable.

But it was more than that. He'd asked about her art therapy work with the veterans and talked about Sammy's TSS in a way that showed her he respected her work and her opinions. They shared a love for Sammy that made their relationship deeper.

She wanted this. Wanted to explore a relationship with Jack and see where it would go.

She wanted desperately to tell him the truth about Sammy. That secret was the only thing standing between them, but it was huge.

Tell him tonight.

But telling him tonight could, and probably would, ruin tonight.

And how could she tell him the truth, breaking Chloe's trust, when she was wearing Chloe's dress?

"Sit tight. I'll get your door." Jack jumped out and came around to open her door.

Oh, those gentlemanly manners, so rare in a guy her age. And Jack was so handsome in his dark suit and tie. He could have been a model in an ad for expensive cars or luxury vacations.

You sure couldn't be a model.

She shoved away the automatic negative thought as she took his hand and let him help her out of the car. She knew she looked fine in the dress, and her hair wasn't *too* crazy.

"Did I tell you how great you look?" he asked as they walked across the parking lot toward the stately old hotel.

"Thanks." She waved a hand at the dress. "Chloe had terrific fashion sense."

Now what had possessed her to say such an idiotic thing? She shot a sideways glance at him and saw an odd expression cross his face. "Actually," he said, "I picked out that dress as a gift for her."

"But it still had the tags on it."

"She didn't like it."

"Oh." She pondered what that meant. Why wouldn't Chloe have liked this dress?

But it wasn't hard to figure out. Chloe had liked more subdued colors and classic styles.

If Jack, conservative, orderly Jack, had picked out this dress…well, that was something else they had in common.

Flustered, she looked off toward the mountains where the sun was sinking into a pink-and-orange streak of clouds. "It's a gorgeous night."

"It'll be cool later. And you didn't bring a wrap." Jack sounded chagrined. "You can wear my jacket."

Sweet Jack. She squeezed his arm tighter. "Is Sammy going to be okay with Mrs. Jennings tonight?"

"Yes, he's fine. She's been wanting to mend fences, and I figured tonight would be a good time, since we're close by." He greeted the doorman and ushered her inside with a hand on her back.

Arianna tried not to make too much of his touch, but her heart was pounding.

She greeted Penny, resplendent in her new dress, her hair in an updo that made her look incredibly sophisticated. As the owner and manager of the ranch, she was the public face of the fund-raiser, and she was obviously up to the task, greeting everyone, directing the staff, looking over the food and the silent auction.

Branson Howe watched her admiringly.

"I'm going to see if she needs any help," Arianna said and escaped from Jack before he could answer. She needed space to breathe, because being near him was sweeping her way too far away from anything like clear thinking.

"What can I do to help?" she asked as soon as she reached her friend's side.

Penny hugged her. "Don't even think about helping," she said. "You be a guest." She held Arianna at arm's length and studied her. "You look absolutely stunning."

"You clean up pretty well yourself. Hard to believe we were scrubbing kennels this morning." Arianna had started volunteering in the kennels a couple of hours a week. She took Buster and let him play with the other puppy who was still living there while she did whatever was needed with the senior dogs. The only problem was that she wanted to take all of them home. She was pretty sure she'd end up with at least one once Buster was a little older.

If she stayed around.

She turned to look for Jack and saw him talking intently with an older man in a suit.

Oh. It was Jack's father.

Her stomach sank. For whatever reason, the man really disliked her. She'd always felt judged by him, as if he could see right through her.

She turned away in search of someone else to talk to and was happy to see Daniela, looking lovely in a cream-colored dress, her pregnancy now more obvious. "You look gorgeous!" Arianna hugged her.

Daniela touched her scarred face in what looked like an automatic gesture, and Arianna's heart twisted. Daniela really *was* gorgeous, and her scars didn't detract from that.

Her husband, Gabe, wrapped his arms around her from behind, and Daniela's eyes and smile lit up her face, making her glow.

If only Jack could be so affectionate with Arianna. But even if their relationship were close enough to merit that, he couldn't show such physical demonstration in front of his father.

He was approaching now, and her heartbeat quickened, because he was looking at her almost the same way Gabe had looked at Daniela. He reached her side and greeted Gabe and Daniela, casually putting an arm around Arianna's shoulders.

She saw Gabe's eyebrow lift, just slightly. Daniela tilted her head and narrowed her eyes, looking at Arianna.

Arianna looked over at Jack. "Your dad's not going to like this."

He smiled down at her with all the confidence and certainty in the world. "His problems are his own, not mine."

She swallowed. "Oh."

His eyes held hers for a long moment, and then he smiled, a dimple showing in his cheek. "Come on, let's go look at the food. I'm starving."

Arianna had been hungry, too, until Jack had looked at her in that intense way. Now her stomach felt so fluttery that she didn't know if she could eat.

He still had his arm around her. He was being public about the fact that this was a date.

She had to tell him the truth, and soon. She'd promised Chloe she wouldn't, but everything had changed. Now that she'd forged a relationship with Jack and Sammy, keeping the secret had the potential to devastate both of them.

Her new friend Lily came up behind them. "You've got to try those little tarts," she said, indicating one of the many trays of food. "They're some kind of seafood and cheese, and they taste amazing."

"And high calorie," Arianna said. "You can afford it. I can't."

"You look fantastic. And don't you know that when you're at an event for a good cause, the calories don't count?"

"Second the motion that you look fantastic," Jack growled into her ear.

Her stomach fluttered again, but she gathered a small plate of appetizers and sat with Jack at one of the high tables that dotted the room. Along one wall, silent auction items were meeting with a lot of attention, mostly baskets of luxury goods, some pet items and a couple of handmade blankets.

After the crowd had mingled and eaten for a while, Penny took the podium and got everyone's attention.

"Thank you all so much for coming out to support Redemption Ranch," she said. "We're mostly going to let you enjoy the evening in a lighthearted way, but I've asked a couple of folks who have benefited from our services to tell you a little bit about what the ranch has meant to them."

There was polite applause, and then when Gabe, who'd grown up around here and earned a number of medals for his wartime bravery, approached the stage, the applause grew warmer.

"I was a wreck when I came to Redemption Ranch," he said, and the applause and murmurs died down. "Even my family was ready to give up on me. It was my last chance."

He pulled out a handkerchief and wiped his forehead. "It meant so much to me, it helped me so much, that I agreed to speak despite being terrified of public speaking." A sympathetic laugh went through the crowd.

He told about how he'd come to the ranch with severe PTSD and little desire to live, and how the ranch's counselors—here he looked at Daniela, who smiled back at him—had given him hope that life would get better.

"But in addition to the counselors," he said, "there was other help available at the ranch, help that really cemented my healing." He turned and spoke to someone just out of sight in the wings and whistled, and two dogs ran to him on the stage. One was a giant black dog, the other a tiny Chihuahua, and when they reached Gabe, he knelt to greet them with obvious affection.

He took the dogs through a few tricks and then sent them to the handler at the edge of the stage and explained how the animals helped the veterans, and vice versa.

Arianna was thoroughly charmed, and she could tell from the smiles around her that many other guests felt the same.

Penny was glowing, which made Arianna happy. Penny deserved to have success at the ranch after everything she'd gone through. She didn't express rancor toward her ex-husband, who'd absconded with the ranch's funds and its executive assistant, but Arianna could tell the whole situation still tasted bitter to the older woman.

Tonight illustrated the admonition that living well was the best revenge, and Arianna was fiercely glad Penny was living well.

Penny came to the stage again as the applause for Gabe finally died down. "Now, even though they don't want us to, we want to thank our key donors," she said. "We'd like to ask each of them to come briefly to the stage. First, we have Branson Howe, president of our local branch of Western States Bank!" He ducked to the stage smiling awkwardly. "Next we have Marge Springer, owner of Mountain Malamutes!" The woman who'd helped with painting Arianna's apartment joined them. "And finally, our major donor, Esperanza Springs' favorite veterinarian, Jack DeMoise!"

Jack growled beside her. "I told her not to do this," he muttered, then made his way to the front of the room and trotted up the steps to the stage.

"Speech," someone called.

The three onstage looked at each other, and Branson and Marge gestured toward Jack.

Good-naturedly, he took the microphone. "I don't like public speaking any better than Gabe does," Jack said. "And I didn't get the chance to practice, so I'll just say…it's a good cause. And everyone should come up to the ranch and find a senior dog to adopt." To general applause and laughter, he added, "And that's as long as I'm going to keep you away from your food and drinks and dancing."

Arianna was proud of him as he came down from the stage and wove his way through the crowd toward her, exchanging friendly greetings with dozens of people along the way. "I didn't know," she said when he returned.

"You're not supposed to." He held out his hands to her as the music started up again. "Would you like to dance?"

She sighed. Would she?

She wanted nothing more than to dance with Jack. And she'd resigned herself to the fact that this night wasn't the time she was going to be able to tell him the truth about Sammy. So she let him lead her to the dance floor and guide her gently through a semislow dance.

Whatever else happened, she'd have this night to remember.

"Are you having fun?" he murmured in her ear.

"Yes."

"I am, too," he said. "Arianna, I—"

A hand on her arm that wasn't Jack's made her open her eyes. She blinked at Mr. DeMoise. "For Chloe's sake," he said in a too-loud whisper, "could the two of you stop making a spectacle of yourselves?"

* * *

When Jack saw the hurt expression on Arianna's face, fury flashed through him, quick and hot. He gripped his father by the shoulders, hard, and physically moved him away from Arianna as he stepped in between them.

An expression something like fear came into his father's eyes.

Immediately, Jack dropped his hands from his father. He turned and scanned the crowd, noticing in a distant way that a number of people seemed to be watching. He caught Daniela's eye and beckoned her over. "Could you keep Arianna company for a few minutes?" he asked. "I need to speak with my father outside."

"Of course." She put an arm around Arianna, who looked ready to cry.

Jack took his father's arm and steered him toward the exit. Dad had regained his composure and was blustering and resisting with every step.

"I'd like to speak to you privately." Jack continued urging his father forward. "What I have to say isn't pretty, and I would rather not say it in front of other people, for your sake. But I also am not going to physically force you outside. It's your choice." Again, he dropped his hand from his father. Dad looked at him, pressed his lips tight together, nodded once and led the way outside.

They managed to reach the parking lot before boiling over.

"I've put up with a lot from you over the years," Jack said. "But I will not accept you speaking disrespectfully to my friends."

"Friends? Is that what Arianna is to you? Somehow I doubt it."

Dad's snide, angry tone fanned the flames of Jack's

anger. "What possible business is it of yours what my relationship with Arianna might be?"

"I don't like to see you making a fool of yourself in front of the whole community," Dad said. "And I don't like to see you disrespecting your late wife's memory."

"Dancing with a kind, good woman isn't making a fool of myself," Jack said. He drew in a couple of deep breaths and reminded himself that this was his father and he needed to show respect. "Look, I understand that it may feel uncomfortable because Arianna is Chloe's sister. Believe me, I wouldn't have chosen to be drawn to someone related to Chloe, but it happened. I have to believe God has a reason for it."

"Oh, don't bring God into this," Dad said. "Chloe knew what was going on between you two, and she hated it. There's nothing godly about adultery."

Jack stared. "You think I was committing *adultery*? You really think I'm the type of person who would do that?"

"I understand the temptations, son." His father looked away. "I'm trying to keep you from making the same mistakes I made."

"Whoa, whoa, whoa." Jack drew in a slow breath and let it out, staring at his father, who was still not meeting his eyes. "Really, Dad?"

His father didn't nod, but he didn't deny it. Jack's parents' strained relationship appeared in his mind's eye, a picture in a whole new frame. "That's something separate that you need to deal with," he said. "If there's something you need forgiven for, Carson can talk to you or recommend a counselor." Even as he was talking reasonably, Jack's heart ached for his mother. He'd known his parents hadn't had a good marriage, but he had never known why.

His father crossed his arms and looked out across the parking lot. Everything in his posture said he didn't want to talk about it, didn't want to be here with Jack.

Fine. "For now," Jack said, "I insist that you keep your negativity to yourself and don't spew it out over Arianna or me or anyone else I know. It sounds like you've got some thinking to do."

"You mean to tell me this thing between you and Arianna just started up?"

"There's not a *thing* between me and Arianna," Jack said. "She was my sister-in-law, and she's Sammy's aunt and nanny. I care about her a great deal, and I would like to pursue a relationship with her, but that hasn't happened yet. I don't know how she feels about it."

"I can tell you how she feels about it," Dad said. There was some kind of bitterness in his tone. "She looks at you like you're the king of the universe."

Really? That notion spread warmth through Jack's heart.

"Nobody ever looked at me like that," his father added.

Jack spread his hands. "I'm just a man, struggling to raise my son and do my work and follow God's laws," he said. "I'm not going to deny that I've made mistakes. I'm not going to claim that Chloe and I had the perfect marriage. We didn't." He looked upward at the stars. "If I'm fortunate enough to be in a relationship again, I hope I can do better. And I would appreciate it if you didn't interfere with that."

His father didn't answer, but he gave the tiniest of nods.

Jack's emotions spun from hope about Arianna to hurt

about what he'd just learned about his father. "Thanks," he said, then turned on his heel and walked back inside.

Then, because his father was aging and upset, he approached Carson. "Calling in a favor, man," he said. "My dad is out in the parking lot, and he's...troubled. Any chance that you could talk to him a little and make sure he gets home okay?"

"You've got it. I'll take him home myself. Lily isn't here, and I don't like to stay out too late when she's home alone."

Jack met his friend's eyes. "I hope you know how good you've got it."

"I do." Carson clapped him on the back and then headed outside.

Jack found Arianna sitting with Daniela on a bench at the side of the room, partially hidden behind some potted palms. He gripped her hands and pulled her to her feet, and she ended up closer than he'd expected. He had the strongest urge to pull her in and kiss her.

From the way she sucked in her breath and stared at him, she might have let him.

But Daniela was here, and so were a lot of other people. He didn't want to embarrass her that way. "Can we talk?" he asked.

"And that would be my cue to leave the premises," Daniela said. "I've left poor Gabe alone too long. He doesn't like this kind of event."

After she walked away, he looked down at Arianna.

She was studying him. "Are you okay?"

"Exactly what I was going to ask you," he said. "Look, I'm really sorry about my dad. He's dealing with some things I wasn't aware of, but that's no excuse for him being rude to you."

She bit her lip. "Do *you* think we were making fools of ourselves?"

He lifted his hands, palms up. "No doubt there are some people who noticed us dancing together. Some of them know that you are Chloe's sister. Some of them will gossip about that." He took her hand. "But life is short, and I won't live it worried about what people will think. As long as I feel that I'm right with God, that I'm doing my best to be honest and kind and to do the right thing, then I want to move ahead."

She'd been looking at him when he had started talking, but now her eyes dropped. "I want to do the right thing, too," she said. She drew in a deep, shuddering breath. "And that's why there's something I need to tell you."

Chapter Twelve

Tell him now. You have to tell him now.

A sharp knife of dread lodged itself in Arianna's throat. She coughed past it, ruthlessly. "Jack, I—"

"Let's go somewhere more private," he interrupted. He put an arm around her shoulders and guided her toward a back doorway. "There's a little courtyard out here, and I don't think anyone from the gala has discovered it."

Relief washed over her at the brief reprieve, and then her anxiety thrummed back even louder. No matter how beautiful the spot, she was about to tell him something ugly.

Oh, Sammy's birth wasn't ugly. Any baby was a blessing, and Sammy felt like a special one. His adoption, too, was a beautiful thing.

But the cover-up, the fact that Jack had been raising Sammy for eighteen months, unaware of her and Chloe's conspiracy of silence… That was ugly and that was a mistake.

"Here we go." Jack led her out into a cool green oasis. Small trees surrounded a tiled courtyard. In the center was a fountain with burbling water and two small benches. Some night-flowering plant scented the air.

Arianna was praying now. *Please, God, give me the right words. Help me explain in a way that does the least damage to Sammy, to Jack and to Chloe.*

The thought of her sister made guilt rise up in her. *I'm sorry, Chloe. I couldn't keep the secret.* She was picturing her sister's face, sad and anxious and judgmental.

Jack drew her to a bench and tugged gently at her hand. "Sit down," he said. "Now, what's this big secret you have to tell me?" His tone was indulgent.

She looked into his kind eyes and tried to memorize their tender expression, because she didn't think it was going to last much longer.

"If you keep looking at me like that," he began, brushing a stray strand of hair back from her face, letting his thumb trail along her cheek, "I'm not going to be responsible for what happens."

Her heartbeat accelerated. "Chloe—"

"Shh." He touched a fingertip to her lips. "I've made my peace with Chloe and how she'd feel about us being together. She's in such a better place now, I can't think she'd begrudge us happiness."

He leaned forward and gently brushed his lips across hers, releasing a tsunami of emotions inside her. Her heart cried out with longing to melt into his kiss.

It was the love and acceptance she'd always longed for. Jack knew her, had known her for years now, and he cared for her, wanted to kiss her. And not just to kiss her, but to be close in every way, a closeness of the heart and mind.

She tried to hold on to reason. The further she let this go forward, the worse the truth would be when it came out. Pulling back, she extracted herself from his arms and turned away. "I mean it, Jack. Remember when you and Chloe were trying so hard to adopt, and it wasn't happening because of her issues with anxiety and depression? Until finally, the agency let you know that they had a baby for you?"

His phone pinged, and he held up a hand. "Hold that thought. I have my phone on Do Not Disturb, except for Mrs. Jennings. Let me check what's going on."

Arianna grasped hard at the iron bench. She was launched now. She just had to keep the flow of words coming, and it almost felt like a relief to finally let Jack in on the truth. She waited as he paced a little away, head down, focusing on whatever Mrs. Jennings was saying. "Uh-huh. Did you take his temperature? Oh yes, I hear him." He glanced back at her, mouthed the word *sorry*.

"I'll be right over to pick him up," he said.

"What's wrong?" she asked as he clicked off the phone.

"I don't know. Mrs. Jennings says Sammy is really sick."

"Oh no!" Fresh anxiety cut through her preoccupation with herself. "What's wrong with him?" If something happened to Sammy, if he got sick…it didn't bear thinking about.

He held out a hand and took hers. "I'm really sorry, but I've got to go. I'm not too worried. Mrs. Jennings tends to overreact, but just on the chance that she's right and he's picked up something serious, I'm going to head over." They were walking rapidly back the way they'd come. They reached the door and he held it for her to walk inside. "Look, I'm sure you can get a ride home with Daniela or Penny. Stay and enjoy yourself."

As if. "No," she said. "I'm coming with you."

"You're sure?"

"Of course. I'm worried about him."

They made their way through the crowd and out to Jack's car, and Arianna's mind raced the whole time.

What if Sammy were sick enough to go to the hospital, and she couldn't even visit him because she wasn't thought to be related?

Keep him safe, Father, and I'll tell the truth, no matter what the outcome.

"We're almost there." Jack considered running the last red light before the hospital. He decided he could wait rather than potentially explaining himself to a police officer, resulting in more time wasted. "How's he look?"

Sammy wasn't bellowing out his usual wail; instead, he just let out a series of small, fussy bleats that almost broke Jack's heart.

"He's still pale and feverish," Arianna said from the back seat. "And... Oh no, he just threw up. It's okay, honey, it's okay. We'll get you cleaned up." Looking in the rearview, Jack could see her digging through the diaper bag, finding wipes, cooing at Sammy the whole time.

Jack checked the intersection carefully and then gunned through the red light. He swung into the parking lot of the hospital and looked around wildly. He'd never been here before, never had need. Sammy was normally as healthy as a horse, and so was Jack himself.

There, a red sign: Emergency Room. He turned toward it with a squeal of tires, and a moment later, they were at the door of the ER. He jammed the car into Park and jumped out.

Arianna unfastened Sammy from the car seat and

handed him out to Jack. "I'll go park the car and then be right behind you."

"Thanks." He didn't know what he'd have done without her. Mrs. Jennings had gotten worried because, in addition to him having a fever, Sammy's diaper had been dry for hours. Initially, that hadn't seemed like such a big deal to him, but seeing Sammy's dull fussiness, feeling his high fever, he was getting a much more serious set of worries.

He carried Sammy inside—man, he was burning up—and rushed a lackadaisical clerk through infuriatingly slow intake procedures. Arianna hurried in just as the med techs came to get Sammy.

They wanted to put him on a gurney. But Sammy wailed and clung to Jack. "I'll carry him in," Jack said and headed toward the double doors.

"Sir, our procedure dictates that—"

Arianna sped up to interrupt, walking alongside the tech who seemed to be in charge. "He has autism. Change bothers him, and he has sensory issues. He can't be separated from his dad."

"Ma'am, what's your connection to this child?"

"She's his aunt and she takes care of him, and he needs her in here," Jack said over his shoulder. Then they were in a cubicle and everything moved in double time: an IV and blood tests—horrific trying to find Sammy's vein—and then waiting for the chest X-ray and renal ultrasound.

"Why are they testing his lungs and kidneys?" Arianna was holding Sammy now, rocking him gently back and forth, and Jack gave information to the doctors and then paced.

"The fact he hasn't been urinating. There might be something wrong with his kidneys. The chest X-ray…

heart, lungs, bones, there's a lot they can see from it."
He blew out a panicky breath, trying not to think about
the radiation and its effect on a baby like Sammy. Right
now, they had to find out what was wrong, and fast.

Somehow they got through the tests, and the IV
started to help with his blood volume and electrolyte
balance. Sammy was admitted to a private room in the
pediatric unit—not the ICU, for now—and the sun had
already risen over the hospital parking lot when the pediatric ER doctor finally came in with the test results. He
checked Sammy over visually and looked at the moni-
tors, but didn't wake him.

"He's stable for now," the doctor said then, pulling
up a chair to sit knee to knee with Jack and Arianna in
the room, crowded with machinery and supplies. "But
this is serious."

"What's going on?" Jack's heart felt like it was going
to fly out of his chest. It was only natural to take Arianna's hand and squeeze it tightly. He felt like he was
holding on to a lifeline.

"He seems to have gone into renal failure."

Jack's stomach hollowed out, and emptiness filled
him. His lungs felt empty, too, like he'd run a long race;
it was hard to catch his breath.

The doctor looked from Jack to Arianna and then
perched reading glasses on the end of his nose and
looked down at the sheaf of test results in his hands.
"Right now we don't know why, and figuring that out
will help determine our course of treatment. He's going
to be here a few days, I would think. But this could be
the beginning of a long process."

As long as the doctor was talking about beginnings
rather than endings. He slowed his breathing deliber-

ately. He had to hold it together. What he wanted was to take Sammy in his arms and hold him tight, but the poor kid was sleeping, finally, and Jack wouldn't indulge himself by waking him up. He reached over and patted his son's blanket-covered foot instead. "Renal failure," he repeated, trying to take it in, to understand it.

"He's going to be okay?" Arianna sounded as desperate as Jack felt himself.

"I hope so," the doctor said, which wasn't exactly the reassuring answer Jack wanted to hear. "Do you know if he's ingested anything new in the past twenty-four, forty-eight hours? Chewed on something, gotten into some medicine?"

"I don't think so," Jack said, and Arianna frowned and shook her head. "He's been with one of us constantly until tonight, and he was with a dependable babysitter tonight." Guilt suffused him at leaving Sammy with Mrs. Jennings. He didn't suspect her of leaving Sammy unsupervised, but if he'd been with his son himself, he might have noticed symptoms sooner.

"The other question is genetic," the doctor said. "For two reasons. One, is there any history of kidney disease in either of your families? And two…" He met their eyes again. "Is there a potential donor, if it should come to that? Which could include either of you."

Jack sucked in a breath.

"A *kidney* donor?" Arianna sounded as shocked as Jack felt. "Is that…likely? Is it that bad?"

"We just don't know yet. If it's needed, we'd want it to happen quickly, and that's why I'm bringing up the subject now." He reached over and patted Sammy's foot just as Jack had done. "I certainly hope not, and there's

a good chance that he'll clear whatever infection or tox-
icity is causing the problem and be just fine."

Jack shook his head slowly. "He's adopted," he said.
"Closed adoption. I can petition to have the records
opened for medical reasons, but there's time and paperwork involved."

"Definitely get it started." The doctor frowned. "I'd
like to see the family history ASAP."

Arianna let out a choked sound.

Jack and the doctor both turned to her, and Jack
squeezed her hand.

Her breathing was rapid, her eyes huge, staring at
Sammy.

"Are you okay?" Jack asked.

At the same time, the doctor patted her hand. "I know
it's a lot to take in."

She cleared her throat and looked at the doctor. "I
can actually answer those questions," she said. "About
his genetics?" Her face was almost as white as the doctor's jacket.

"You're the aunt, correct?" The doctor consulted his
records and then looked expectantly at Arianna.

"Ye-e-e-s," she said, drawing out the word. "I'm his
adoptive aunt. But I have some information about his
genetic background."

Jack had been holding her hand all this time, but
now he dropped it, turned and studied her. What was
she talking about?

Her gaze flickered over to him and then back to the
doctor. "Sammy doesn't have any biological relatives
with kidney disease," she said, speaking slowly and
clearly, kind of like a person who'd had too much to
drink and was trying to sound sober. "And he does have

at least one direct relation who's willing to be tested as a donor if it becomes necessary."

Her words made no sense. "Arianna," Jack said, "how can you know that?"

The doctor looked up from his chart.

Arianna met Jack's eyes and took his hand again, swallowed convulsively. "I know it," she said, "because I'm his biological mother."

Jack stared at her. "What?"

She nodded. "I carried him and birthed him," she said. "He's my son."

Jack's world, as he knew it, seemed to spin faster and faster until it exploded.

Chapter Thirteen

Arianna's heart raced, and her palms were sweating. At the same time, it was as if a giant boulder she'd been trying to hold in place had finally crashed down the mountainside. There might be massive destruction in its wake, but at least she could stop this ceaseless effort to keep it in place.

Jack's face was expressionless, his voice toneless. "That can't be true."

The doctor looked from her to Jack. "This is something you were unaware of?"

He shook his head, quick and hard. "Arianna, I'm sure you feel like his mother at times, especially since you've been taking care of him, but Sammy's adoption was closed."

"Yes, I know," she said and swallowed. "Chloe and I decided that was best."

"What?" Jack's word exploded from him like a gunshot.

Best to get it all out at once. "Chloe couldn't have a child, and I got pregnant and knew I couldn't raise one," she said, the words tumbling over each other. "It seemed to make sense at the time, if she raised my child."

Jack was staring at her. "This is no time for jokes."

She tried to breathe slowly, to calm herself down. But it was next to impossible, because this mattered so much, mattered almost more than anything had ever mattered in her life. *Jack* mattered, and every word from her mouth was hurting him, stabbing him, cutting him. Cutting apart their relationship, this sweet, precious thing that had just started to grow. "It's not a joke. I'm sorry."

"You're sorry. You're *sorry*?"

The doctor cleared his throat and closed the file folder. "Well. I have the preliminary answers I needed regarding the boy's genetics, if this…ah…*revelation* proves to be true. We'll keep a close eye on Sammy and keep running tests. I'll be back in the afternoon." He stood, his legs knocking his chair backward into some equipment, making a metallic clang.

Jack nodded distractedly. "Thank you."

"Thanks." Ariana glanced up at the man and then looked away from his curious frown.

They waited while the doctor left the room. At the doorway, a smiling nurse started to wheel in a cart. "Hey, everyone, another vitals check!" she called out.

The doctor stopped her, speaking in a low voice. She looked past him, curiosity in her eyes, and then backed the cart into the hallway. A little girl's voice rang out and was hushed.

The hospital room's door closed with a gentle swish.

And then Arianna and Jack were alone in the hospital room with Sammy. And the truth.

It wasn't the situation she'd imagined when she'd

thought of telling Jack that she was Sammy's mother. She'd intended to prepare him mentally, sit down in a comfortable, private place. To start at the beginning and explain, carefully, what had happened, what had led to this horrible mess.

Instead, she'd piled a second shock on top of the jolt of Sammy's serious illness. No wonder Jack looked so stunned.

Even though she couldn't fix it, she had to try. "I know it doesn't help, but I'm sorry. So terribly, terribly sorry. Not for having Sammy, and not for placing him with you, but for keeping the secret. Chloe didn't want—"

"Stop." Jack held up a hand as if he could physically halt the flow of words. "I'm trying to take this in."

"Of course. Sorry." She was going about this all wrong. If she could only think of the right words, maybe she could soften the fact that they'd hidden such a vast secret, make it hurt him less.

Sammy stirred in his bed, and they both stood and hurried from the foot of his bed to the side of it. Arianna started to brush aside a wayward strand of Sammy's hair and then pulled back her hand. It wasn't her right. She waited, arms rigidly at her sides, while Jack straightened Sammy's covers.

He was so close that she could smell his aftershave, just a hint of it. Last night that smell had evoked another kind of strong emotion, but that seemed like a century ago.

He moved back to the chairs they'd been sitting in and she followed. She sat, and he moved his chair away from her.

Her heart was breaking, cracking in two.

He stared at the floor for a long time, and she watched him, forcing herself to stay quiet, to let him process the news in his own way. Finally, he looked up at her. "Chloe knew the whole time? And kept it from me?"

She nodded, and he looked away.

This was a third awful thing he had to deal with: the fact that his marriage hadn't been what he thought, that there had been a huge lie at the center of it. He didn't betray much with his expression, but a muscle twitched in his cheek.

"Why?" he asked in a low tone.

Here was her chance to explain. To find the words that would give him a little bit of peace, and that might allow her to still see Sammy, be there for him, at least a little. She chose them carefully.

"Do you remember when I went to Atlanta to live for a few months, and Chloe came to visit me? Did that seem a little odd to you?"

He nodded.

"Right, because we weren't that kind of close sisters. But she'd found out from our mother that I was expecting a baby."

He looked up quickly. "Whose baby?"

Oh, she didn't want to go there. She knew instinctively that finding out Sammy's paternity would be a blow to Jack. "Let me tell the story in my way?" she asked. "I'll get to all of it. I promise."

He nodded. He still wasn't meeting her eyes, and that was killing her. She wanted to sink down onto her knees and beg for forgiveness, to cry on his shoulder— anything to keep their connection alive. She reached for his hand.

He crossed his arms and turned, avoiding her touch. "Just tell it."

"Okay." She drew in a deep breath, let it out and started talking. "She came to ask me if she could adopt the baby. My plan had always been to place the baby for adoption. Well, almost always." She'd thought, at first, that maybe she and Nathan could marry and raise their child. But when she'd met Nathan for coffee, planning to tell him about her pregnancy and discuss what to do, he'd beaten her to the punch, telling her he didn't want to be involved with her anymore and that he'd gotten a wonderful postdoc up in Boulder, one that didn't pay well but would allow him to do his research.

She remembered looking at him, this man she liked but didn't love, this man whose bright future would be crushed by the requirement to support her and a child. She'd shot up a desperate prayer to a God she barely knew.

The next moment, a family had come into the restaurant, a Caucasian mother and father and a little girl with Asian features. "Can I have a milkshake, Mama?" the girl had asked.

The man had swung her up high, making her giggle, and then settled her into his arms. "Whatever you want, princess," he'd said.

Arianna didn't consider herself to be a true Christian back then. She'd only just started going to church again after several years away. But even she could recognize a divine moment. It was as if God had proffered a visual aid, just when she needed it: *adoption can be the perfect answer.*

"It's okay, Nathan," she'd said. "You've got to follow your dreams. I understand."

Now she looked at Jack, his shoulders hunched and tight, lines bracketing his downturned mouth. In trying to do the right thing by Nathan and Chloe and, most of all, Sammy, she'd done Jack a great wrong. "It seemed to make sense. We were both immature, not good at thinking about future consequences. And for different reasons, we both felt desperate."

He was quiet for a couple of minutes, and then he looked at her, his face bleak. "I get why you and Chloe would've made that arrangement. I guess. But why wouldn't you tell me?"

She lifted her hands, palms up. "Chloe insisted. For reasons she wouldn't explain to me, she didn't want you to know."

"But you knew what Chloe was like!" he burst out. "Why would you let her make a decision like that for you? A decision that was so wrong?"

Why *had* she? Yes, Chloe had been persuasive, and Arianna had been raised to take care of her. But she wouldn't normally have allowed Chloe to lead her into doing something she thought was wrong.

The part she'd barely admitted to herself, the part she'd shoved down and avoided, nudged into the hospital-bright light. "I wanted to know him," she admitted through a throat that had gone thick and achy. "I wanted to see him growing up and to know he was okay. I couldn't face just giving him to strangers, getting a photo once a year."

Jack's mouth tightened. He didn't say anything, but to Arianna, his expression was pure negative judgment.

"Do you know what it was like, going through pregnancy and childbirth, holding him in my arms, loving him more and more, and then letting him go?" Her voice was hoarse and tears were rolling down her face, but she couldn't stop now. "It was like tearing out part of my heart and throwing it aside. It almost killed me, Jack! But it was good for Sammy. And that was what mattered."

Jack was shaking his head. "No. Stop it. I'm not going to feel sorry for you."

"Of course not," she choked out. "That's not what I want, I was just trying to explain—"

"You came to me and offered to be his nanny," he said. "Knowing you were his mother. You've hung out with me and eaten meals with me and—" He broke off, looking at her with eyes that expressed pure pain, and she knew what he had been about to say.

She'd kissed him. Knowing this awful secret, she'd kissed him.

"Were you planning to try to get him back? Is that why you acted like you cared for me?"

"No, Jack, of course not. I wanted to tell you—"

"But you didn't, did you?" He swallowed and straightened. "Get out."

"What?" She met his eyes, saw the anger there and instinctively crossed her arms over her chest.

He waved a hand at the door. "Go on. I don't want you here."

"But Sammy needs—"

"I'm still his father," Jack interrupted, his voice hard and cold. "And I don't want you here."

She stood. "I understand, Jack, but I hope—"

"Now, please?" His voice cracked a little on the last word.

"Okay." She nodded rapidly, then looked over at Sammy. "Will you…" She wanted him to keep her updated, but that wasn't a favor she could ask, not now. "Can I bring you anything? Clothes, a cell phone charger? Coffee?"

"I'll get Penny or Willie to help." He turned away from her and went to Sammy's bedside. His shoulders were stiff and square, a wall against her.

"Right." She swallowed hard and headed out the door.

She had her hand on the door when he said, "Hey."

"Yeah?" She turned back, searching his face for any kind of softening, a hope of forgiveness.

There was none. "You didn't tell me who Sammy's dad is."

Right. And she'd promised to tell him everything. And his attitude toward her was already about as low as it could go. "It was Nathan," she said.

His mouth twisted to the side, and he gave one nod. Looked away from her and waved her out with one hand, as if she were a pesky courtier and he were the king.

She couldn't fault him for it, though. He'd had shock upon shock. "He didn't know, Jack," she said. "Not until he figured it out himself, just a little while ago. Don't hate him."

His lips flattened and he planted his legs wide, his fists clenching. "Do I have to call hospital security to get you out of here?"

It wasn't fair, when he'd asked her a question that had held up her departure. But what she'd done was much, much more unfair. She opened her mouth to say goodbye, couldn't squeeze out the word and half stumbled into the bright corridor, feeling like her own heart had been surgically excised.

Jack got through the next few hours on the kind of autopilot he'd perfected doing long, complex surgeries on extremely fragile animals. He comforted Sammy when he woke up, tried to get him to eat the unfamiliar soft food diet and called Penny to bring in the blue-and-white-checked bear and a few other supplies. He didn't ask it, but she also brought a change of clothes for Jack.

"You should have called the moment this happened," she scolded him. "Honestly, we all thought you and Arianna had gone off for some quiet time together. You seemed like you were having a wonderful night. Where is she, by the way?"

Jack hadn't even thought about the fact that he'd have to explain things to people and figure out who should know the truth about Sammy. For now, he just shook his head. "We had a disagreement," he said.

She'd sat down on the side of Sammy's bed, and at his words, she looked quickly up at him. "That happens," she said, "but I'm sorry it happened now, when there's so much stress in your life. I'm sure you'll work it out."

"No." And he didn't want to talk about it. He sorted through the supplies she'd brought. "Look, Sammy, your cup!"

Sammy reached fretfully for it, then threw it down. He made a fist and rubbed his cheek, then looked expectantly at Jack.

"Does it hurt?" Jack put his hand on Sammy's cheek, then touched his forehead. His fever, thankfully, had gone down.

Sammy twisted away and curled around his bear.

"This has to be hard on him emotionally," Penny said quietly.

Jack nodded. "He doesn't even like it when he has a different food for dinner or gets a new shirt. Being in the hospital means everything is new."

"That's rough. Rough on you, too." Penny patted Jack's arm. "Look, why don't you get a shower and change clothes? I'll sit with Sammy. It looks like he's going to sleep anyway."

"You don't need to…" He trailed off. He wanted to do everything for Sammy himself, but he'd been going nonstop for more than twenty-four hours now. He was just so tired. "Thanks, I will."

After he showered in the little bathroom connected to Sammy's hospital room, and his energy returned, his anger grew. What had Arianna and Chloe been thinking, keeping the truth about Sammy from him? How disrespectful could you get? Had they never intended to tell Sammy, either? What was supposed to happen if Sammy got sick or, when he got older, wanted to know something about his heritage? Had they even considered those ramifications?

Moments from his years with Chloe pushed their way into his head. How brokenhearted she'd been about her infertility. How she'd closed down, turned away from him. How, when they'd adopted Sammy, it hadn't made her as happy as he'd expected it to.

How she'd avoided Arianna, felt competitive with her, been obsessed with the idea that Jack had feelings for her.

Looking at his face in the mirror as he shaved, he almost felt like she was a shadow behind him, hovering. Permanently unhappy.

She'd been beautiful, outwardly perfect. They'd wanted the same things when they'd married. But life hadn't worked out the way they'd planned.

Chloe had struggled with so many issues. He wanted to feel angry with her for her secrecy and lies, but he ran out of gas when he thought it through. She hadn't had full control of her thinking.

But Arianna did! Arianna, free-spirited, warmhearted Arianna, knew perfectly well what she was doing. She'd betrayed him without a second thought, had then come to be his nanny and acted like she was falling for him.

Had she done that because she wanted to get close to Sammy again, to be his mother?

He rammed his fist against the wall of the bathroom. It hurt, but not as much as his heart did.

He'd been falling for Arianna, hard. He'd *wanted* something to happen with her. He'd loved how warm and creative she was with Sammy. He'd even thought of marriage.

What a fool he'd been.

When he came back to Sammy's bedside, refreshed in body if not in spirit, Penny rose to meet him. "They came in and took his vitals, but he's sleeping again," she said. "And your phone's blowing up."

He checked on Sammy, pulled the covers up and stroked his sweaty head. His throat tightened. *It's just you and me, little guy. We'll make it alone.*

Then, to escape his emotions, he scrolled through his phone. For every message from a friend—because word had gotten out in Esperanza Springs, and everyone was worried about Sammy—there was a message from Arianna.

I'm sorry.

Do you need anything?

How is Sammy doing?

Her concern rang so false that he felt like throwing his phone across the room. Instead, he clicked into his phone settings and blocked her number.

Sammy stirred, and his eyes opened. He rubbed his cheek with his fist again.

"I don't know why he keeps doing that," Jack said to Penny. "What's wrong, buddy? Does your face hurt?"

"Oh! I think I know what it is," Penny said unexpectedly.

He looked at her, surprised. "What do you mean?"

"It's a sign. You know how Arianna taught him *more* and *milk* and *banana*?"

And *daddy*. She'd taught him to tap his forehead with the thumb of an open hand, asking for Daddy. He remembered when Arianna had pointed to Jack, and Sammy had half smiled and made the sign.

Arianna had swooped down on him with hugs, her eyes shiny with happy tears. When she'd calmed down a little, she'd explained the sign's significance to Jack.

It had made him feel hopeful. Sammy was learning to communicate. And he was communicating about people, being social. A double win.

In a way, it was Sammy's first time of saying, "Daddy." He remembered how he'd reached over and squeezed Arianna's hand, all full of emotion, and she'd smiled at him.

"So what does the cheek-rub sign mean? Do you know?" Because no way, no *way* was he calling Arianna to find out.

She nodded. "It's his sign for Arianna," she said. "He wants her."

Chapter Fourteen

Sammy was crying. Again.

Arianna stared out the window of her second-floor apartment, looking at the house where Jack and Sammy lived. They'd come home from the hospital last night, but Arianna had no way of knowing how he was doing healthwise. It had been three days since she'd revealed the truth to Jack in the hospital, and she hadn't been able to contact him since.

She could tell Sammy wasn't doing well emotionally. The fussy, whiny sound of his wailing made her ache to comfort him.

She'd go over there. She picked up her purse, got the plate of cookies she'd baked in the hopes of seeing Sammy and started out the door. But two steps down the stairs, she lost her courage.

Jack didn't want her there. He wasn't answering her calls or texts. He had as much as threatened to call hospital security to keep her away. If she showed up on his doorstep, he wouldn't open the door. He might even call the state police.

She went back inside, put down her things and sat

at her small kitchen table, staring out at the Sangre de Cristo Mountains, her gaze frequently turning toward Jack's house.

Sammy's cries stopped, and that was a comfort. Jack must have gotten him calmed down.

Thinking about Jack made her stomach twist into impossible knots. She would never forget the look on his face as the truth had sunk in. Shock. Betrayal. Anger. All understandable emotions, and she couldn't fault him for having them. But what had hurt the most was what hadn't been there: the love and caring that had been in his eyes every time he looked at her. Now that was gone. And it wasn't coming back.

She'd been happy about it, enjoyed it. But she hadn't realized how very blessed she was to have it, and how awful it would be when it was withdrawn. It was the acceptance she'd always wanted and never gotten before. Jack had liked her as she was, her messy, disorganized, slightly overweight self. He cared for her, even knowing her flaws.

Except he hadn't known the worst ones. He hadn't known what she was hiding, what she had concealed, and when he had discovered that, it had proven to be too much, even for his larger-than-normal heart.

She'd blown it. She blown the best thing she'd ever had.

The sound of a thin, high cry drifted across the space between the houses on a mountain breeze, quickly increasing in volume. Sammy was upset again.

It was killing her not to know what was going on with him, whether his prognosis was good, whether some kind of a transplant was going to be needed. Oh, she'd gladly give Sammy a kidney or any other organ that she could donate.

If Jack would allow it.

The crying didn't stop. It got louder. She shut the window so she wouldn't hear it anymore. Let him deal with it himself if he was determined to.

She stood with her hands on the window frame, trying to look away.

And then she grabbed her things again and clattered down the stairs. A moment later she was on Jack's front porch, knocking.

He didn't answer.

She knocked again, just a little louder. He had to hear her. She knew he was in there, could hear Sammy's cries distinctly now.

Behind her, she heard a car door slam. Finn, the ranch manager, emerged from the office and walked to meet the suited, cowboy-booted man, who'd apparently come on some sort of business. They walked into the barn.

"Jack! Please, let me come in, just for a minute!"

Sammy's cries escalated.

"Jack! Please!"

The door opened, and there was Jack, stubble thick on his cheeks and lines she'd never seen before bracketing his mouth and crossing his forehead. Dark circles beneath his eyes told the story of sleepless nights.

Sammy's face was red, but he looked far, far healthier than he had when Arianna had last seen him. Relief washed over her, even as his cries grew louder. He reached his little arms toward her.

"You need to leave us alone." Jack's words were clipped. "Seeing you just upsets him more."

"He wants me. If I could just spend a little time with him—"

"That just stretches out his pain." Jack's voice was cold, but his eyes were tortured.

"Look, I know how angry you must be, but we need to talk soon about some kind of an arrangement—"

He held up a hand, shaking his head, cutting her off. "We're not making an arrangement."

She sucked in a shaky breath. "You're not going to let me see him?"

"That's right. It's a closed adoption. You signed away your parental rights."

His words, each distinctly articulated, hammered her like steel.

"I need for you to leave. Now."

Arianna's heart seemed to stretch out toward her son, crying in Jack's arms. She could comfort him, she knew she could. "Please, Jack—"

"Don't make me be cruel."

Still, she stood there, staring, trying to memorize Sammy's little face, to remember what it felt like to hold him in her arms. Trying to memorize Jack's face, too, because she didn't know when she'd see it again.

"Arianna. Go."

She shook her head miserably. "I can't."

Jack closed the door, not with a slam but gently. The click of the lock, though, was decisive.

She stood staring at the closed door for a long moment and then set the cookies down on his porch. She walked back toward her apartment but found she couldn't bear to go back inside. Instead, she headed for a trail that led up into the foothills, walking faster and faster and then running, her throat thick and aching. Soon, tears were pouring down her face, making it hard to see, but she couldn't stop. Couldn't stop moving. Couldn't stop running away from the worst mistake of her life.

It was late afternoon when Arianna came down from the foothills and trudged back to the ranch. Her eyes were dry now. Her soul was dry, too.

She'd had the undeniable urge to just keep walking, walking into the mountain as the night grew colder, as storm clouds gathered. Her purpose in life, whatever purpose she'd had, was gone.

She couldn't see her son. Couldn't help Jack raise him.

She was so overwhelmed with shame and guilt that her forearms kept going across her stomach, as if she were going to fall apart if she didn't literally hold herself together.

Still, some survival instinct brought her back to the ranch. That same instinct told her not to go up to her apartment and spend the evening alone.

She needed help.

She'd poured her soul out to God on that mountain, but God had stayed silent. Maybe she wasn't praying right. She wasn't an experienced Christian.

She wanted to talk to Penny, or maybe to Daniela, but she didn't have Jack's permission to share the story of Sammy, and it wouldn't be right to start telling people something so private. She wouldn't add insult to the injury she'd already done Jack by spreading Sammy's story around town.

But there was one person that she could tell. She got in her car and drove carefully down the mountain road, staying well under the speed limit because she knew how close to the edge she was emotionally. Forty minutes later, she pulled into Pastor Carson Blair's driveway, parked her car and knocked on his front door.

Lily answered. "Arianna! Come in." She peered at Arianna's face. "You look awful. Is Sammy okay?"

Arianna licked dry lips. "Do you think Carson would be willing to talk to me in confidence?"

"Of course he can. Come in." Lily opened the door and ushered her in, then walked her through the house to Carson's study with an arm around her shoulders.

The unquestioning kindness made Arianna's throat thicken with unshed tears.

Lily tapped on the door and spoke to Carson in a low voice, and then he opened the door wider and reached out a hand to Arianna. "Come in. Make yourself comfortable."

Arianna looked at Lily. "This needs to be confidential," she choked out, "but I'd like it if you could stay and hear what I have to say, on those terms."

Lily bit her lip and looked at Carson. "Come help me make some tea and bring in something to eat, and we'll talk about it. Just relax, Arianna, and one or both of us will be right back."

Arianna sat in the comfortable chair in front of Carson's battered desk and let her forehead rest on her hand. She had no idea of what to do, how to handle any of this, but Carson was wise. Carson would help. Carson would pray with her.

There was a snuffling around her legs, and a heavy-set, low-slung dog nosed at her hand. Almost immediately, another equally odd-looking dog rushed in, barking.

"Boomer! No, Boomer!" Sunny, one of Carson's twins, ran in and grabbed the barking dog.

Her sister, Skye, came in, too, and knelt by the quieter dog. She looked up at Arianna, and her head tilted to one side. "I'm sorry you're sad."

"She's sad?" Sunny looked up from her efforts to hold her squirming dog. "Aww. She *is* sad."

The twins looked at each other, seeming to communicate without words. Then Sunny pulled a large dog biscuit out of her pocket and broke it in half.

Instantly, the little dogs sat at attention, silent and alert.

"Now, be quiet. We have to talk to Miss Arianna." Sunny's tone was severe. She handed half of the biscuit to each dog, and they went to opposite corners of the room to eat them.

Still kneeling on the floor, Skye reached up and took Arianna's hand. "I'm sad sometimes, too," she confided.

Not to be outdone, Sunny leaned against Arianna's knees. "Do you need a hug?"

The identical, upturned faces were so full of sweet sympathy that Arianna couldn't help smiling through her tears. "Of course, a hug from you girls would really help," she said, sliding down onto the floor so they could all sit next to each other. The dogs, having finished their biscuits, trotted over and climbed into their three adjoining laps, sniffing pockets, looking for more treats. And then, as the girls told Arianna about their own problems, how they'd started a new school year and were in separate classrooms for the first time, Arianna listened and nodded her sympathy, and a tiny measure of peace rose in her heart.

There was still sweetness and caring in the world. And no, she wasn't going to get the kind she craved, from the person she craved it from, but it still existed, in good friends like Carson and Lily, and in sweet children like Sunny and Skye.

Lily and Carson came back in, Lily carrying a teapot and cups, and Carson a tray piled with cookies and chocolates and cupcakes.

"Girls," Lily said as she set down the teapot, "did you ask if Miss Arianna wanted company? She might need some time alone."

"She doesn't, Mommy," Skye said.

Sunny shook her head. "She's sad, but we made her feel better."

"It's true." Arianna tightened an arm around each girl's shoulders. "They've been so sweet." She wanted to say more, but her voice was catching.

"Actually, girls," Lily said, "there's a new princess movie. For a special treat, would you like to watch it?"

"Yes!" Sunny jumped up.

"Can Miss Arianna watch it, too, with us?" Skye asked.

"No, she needs to talk with Daddy and me," Lily said. "You girls run along. It's all set up, you just have to push Play. And I put a bowl of popcorn up high, where the dogs can't reach it. Will you be very careful to keep the people food away from the dogs?"

Both girls nodded vigorously.

"Okay, then, off you go," Lily said, and the two girls rushed out of the room, the little dogs following after them.

"They are *so* adorable," Arianna said. "And so kind and sweet. And you're such a good mom, Lily."

Lily flushed with obvious pleasure, and Arianna thought about how fully Lily had become a mother to the twins. Indistinguishable from a biological mother, really.

She wondered whether Jack would meet someone

soon, give some woman an opportunity to become a mother to Sammy. It was more than likely; he was a handsome, kind, good man. Any single woman in town would be happy to go out with him.

Her stomach burned at the thought. She didn't want anyone else to fill that role in Jack's life; she wanted to be the one. Had stood a chance of it until he'd found out the truth.

Pastor Carson smiled and took a seat across from her, and Lily sat down at his side, pouring cups of tea. "Why don't you tell us what's going on?" he suggested. "I can see that you're very upset."

So she told them, with a lot of pauses and a few tears. Told them about getting pregnant with Sammy, and about Chloe's proposition, and how she had decided to accept it.

"Why did Chloe want to keep it a secret from her husband?" Lily asked.

"It's complicated," Arianna said. "So complicated that I don't completely understand it. She struggled with some mental health issues, anxiety and depression. And…" She trailed off, thinking.

"Is there something else?" Carson asked gently.

Arianna drew in a breath. "We grew up with a lot of shame," she said slowly. "I've always felt shame about my body, my weight. Chloe didn't have that issue, but I wonder if she was ashamed that her body wouldn't do what she wanted. She couldn't make a baby."

"That could definitely be the case," Lily said. "She could have felt like an inadequate woman."

"There's biblical precedent for that," Carson said. "In ancient cultures, and in some cultures today, unfortunately, a woman's fertility is all tangled up in her sense of worth."

"I could have a baby and she couldn't." Arianna took a cookie and broke it in half. "I never really thought about how jealous that must have made her feel. I was so caught up in what I did wrong, getting pregnant without being married, that I didn't really consider how it must have made Chloe feel." Her heart ached for the sister she'd once been close to. There would be no more opportunity to mend the relationship, to talk about what it had all meant to them. Not on this earth anyway.

Carson and Lily looked at each other. Lily raised an eyebrow, as if asking her husband a question, and Carson gave a nod.

"You may have come to some of the only people who could really understand what you're talking about." Lily took a sip of tea and swallowed. "I kept a big, big secret from Carson when we first met. It had to do with his wife, who was my friend and who died. I thought keeping the manner of her death a secret was a kindness to Carson, but it actually caused us terrible problems."

"I didn't know that." And it made Arianna feel a little better, knowing she wasn't the only person who'd made the mistake of being too secretive.

Lily had even gotten through it and found love and a family.

"Secrets are almost always toxic," Carson said. "Even when they're kept as a mercy to someone else, it almost always backfires."

Arianna nodded. "I know that now. But at that time, I was so desperate, I wasn't thinking straight. Now I hurt Jack so badly. He—" her throat tightened, but she choked it out "—he doesn't want me to ever see Sammy again."

Lily put a hand on Arianna's arm. "Oh, honey, that has to hurt so bad," she said. The sympathy in her voice threatened to open the floodgates of Arianna's heart. She didn't dare speak; she only nodded.

"You know," Carson said, "we all make an awful lot of mistakes in this life. It's part of being human."

Arianna drew in a breath and let it out slowly. "I guess that's true. I hate that I hurt Jack so badly, though, and that…that Sammy will suffer." Again, she had to force the words out through a thick throat. "He keeps crying."

"And Jack won't let you see him?"

She shook her head. "I feel like it can't be fixed. Like it's an impossible situation."

Lily glanced over at her husband, a tiny smile pulling up one corner of her mouth. "Carson kind of specializes in those."

"Correction—Jesus specializes in those." Carson reached for a Bible that sat at the center of his desk. "I'd like to read some Scripture with you, if you don't mind."

Lily patted Arianna's arm. "I need to check on the girls and on dinner," she said. "Will you stay? In fact, why don't you stay the night with us?"

"Oh, I couldn't," she said. "I need to…" Her heart turned over in a low darkness. "Actually, since I'm out of a job, I guess I don't have to do anything."

"Then stay. I'll set an extra place at the table and make sure the guest room has clean sheets."

Arianna spent the next hour with Carson, reading passages he showed her from Scripture. They prayed together, sometimes aloud and sometimes silently. And they talked: about Arianna's childhood, her parents, the things that had led her to get too involved with Nathan.

Every time she felt discouraged, every time she cried, he was able to pull out a Bible passage that addressed what she was feeling. Not that he made her feel bad about crying, but he had real answers.

When Lily knocked and told them that dinner was about ready, Arianna went to the bathroom and splashed her face with water. She felt exhausted, but also clearer and cleaner. The tears she'd cried had been bottled up inside her since way before Jack had gotten angry at her, probably since Sammy's birth. A part of the heavy burden she'd been carrying since then had lifted. *Thank You, Jesus*, she thought. She checked herself in the mirror— impossibly red eyes, but that couldn't be helped—and went out to join the family for dinner.

The dogs begged and the twins were funny, and Carson and Lily were the warmest of hosts. Lily and the girls had made a cake earlier—"Just because," Lily said, "but maybe we sensed you were coming"—and Arianna accepted a big piece without her usual agonizing about her figure.

In the grand scheme of things, looking model perfect didn't matter. Carson and Lily accepted her. God accepted her.

It grieved her deeply that Jack didn't accept her, and that her easy access to Sammy had ended. But with Carson's help, she'd seen that there was a glimmer of a solution. Nothing had ever seemed so unsolvable by human standards, but according to Carson, that was usually where God stepped in.

Lily loaned her toiletries and a nightgown, and she went to bed early, prayed herself to sleep and slept all night without dreams.

Jack hadn't slept well.

Sammy had been up several times, crying. His temperature was normal, and he didn't seem physically sick, other than tired. But he kept making the "Aunt Arianna" sign.

Jack stood up from the breakfast table, where he was attempting to feed Sammy some eggs and toast, and looked out the window. He could tell himself he was looking for Mrs. Jennings, his reluctant substitute baby-sitter for the day. But the truth was, he was checking to see if Arianna had come home.

She hadn't.

Which probably meant she was spending the time with Nathan. Even as he had the thought, one side of himself realized it was irrational. Arianna's relationship with Nathan was in the past. He had believed her when she told him that, and nothing had changed really, not in Arianna and Nathan's relationship.

What had changed was Jack and Arianna's relationship, because she had lied to him.

Nathan was Sammy's father. Arianna was his mother.

He stared bleakly at his son, finally calm and tapping a spoon on the tray of his high chair. He didn't feel any less love for him, knowing his parentage. But the deception hurt.

Not only that, but Arianna and Nathan could so easily be the people raising Sammy, and maybe that would have been better for him. Nathan was incredibly successful on a scale that Jack, a small-town country vet, could never dream of. And Arianna… Well, Arianna was warm and loving and smart and creative, a mother anyone would like to have.

Except for the lying.

The sound of a car engine broke his concentration and he was ashamed of the way his heart rate picked up. Was it her?

But no, it was Mrs. Jennings, and Jack sighed as he looked around his messy home. Sammy's tantrums and meltdowns meant that Jack hadn't had a spare moment to clean up the place. The clutter, the spilled orange juice, the slight diaperish smell—all of it got to him, made him feel uncomfortable in his own home. In his own skin.

He still had feelings for Arianna. He couldn't deny it. But he wasn't going to act on them. Wasn't going to let Sammy start to get reattached to her when she was likely to flit off to another adventure at any moment. They'd only had an agreement for the rest of the summer, and summer was nearly over. He'd been a fool to stop his nanny search, somehow trusting that Arianna would stick around. She wouldn't, and even if she would, he wouldn't have her.

Mrs. Jennings bustled in, full of stories about her grandkids. She set her purse on the floor and took off her jacket without even a slight break in her conversational flow. She'd always been like that, but her rate of speech seemed to have sped up now, and he realized she was nervous. He set out to reassure her, because he really couldn't do without her, not now. She wasn't the best with Sammy, but she was far, far from the worst. Sammy knew her, and that was important.

Mrs. Jennings looked around the room and raised an eyebrow. "I see why you wanted me to take care of him up here," she said. "Looking for a little light cleaning in addition to childcare, are you?"

Jack was too tired to tell if she was joking or seriously annoyed. "I'll pay you extra," he promised, "if you can get the house into its usual shape."

Sammy had gotten down from the table and was crawling directly toward Mrs. Jennings's purse.

"Oh, he loves that thing," she said, laughing. She didn't stop Sammy from reaching inside.

"I'd rather you didn't let him…" Jack trailed off and stared in horror as Sammy pulled out a colorful plastic container and banged it on the floor until it opened. He picked up a small white pill.

"Oh no, Sammy, no, no!" Mrs. Jennings reached down and took the pill and pill container from him. "Those are Mrs. Jennings's special candies."

Jack's insides froze. "Has he done that before?"

She seemed to hear something in his voice. "No, of course not."

"What did you mean, when you said he loves your purse?"

"Oh, well…" Her eyes shifted back and forth, not meeting Jack's. "He just always grabs for it. I'm sure he's never gotten in before."

"You keep your medications locked away at home, right?"

"Yes, I do." She looked indignant. "I take care of my own grandchildren. Do you think I wouldn't keep them safe?"

He hoped she would keep *all* the children in her care safe. "I'm just wondering," he said slowly, "whether Sammy could have gotten ahold of your purse and taken a pill or several."

"No! That's not possible."

"Like he was about to do just now," Jack continued as if she hadn't spoken. "Like he would have done in a second, if we hadn't both been looking at him. I'm just wondering whether his kidney episode could have been because he ingested some medication. That's one of the things the doctor asked about."

"Now you're blaming me for his kidney issues?" Mrs. Jennings grabbed her purse. "I knew I should never have started taking care of him again. You'll just have to find another caregiver, one who's up to your standards."

Yes, he would. "What kinds of medication do you carry with you?"

"Just one kind, and it's my personal business." Her face was pink.

He stepped in front of the door, blocking her way. "If I need to get the police to investigate, I will. This could help the doctors know how to finish treating Sammy."

"It was an antianxiety medication, all right? I don't even remember what it's called. I'll text you the name of it. Now, let me through!"

He did let her through and watched as she got into her car and floored it, gravel flying under her tires.

So the mystery of Sammy's kidney problem might very well be solved. Too bad there was only one person he wanted to share that knowledge with. And he'd barred her from ever again coming over or speaking to his son.

Her son.

Chapter Fifteen

An hour later, Jack sat out on his front porch with Sammy, but *not* because he wanted to see Arianna. No, he was sitting there because he was at the end of his rope, with Sammy and with life generally, and sometimes being outside kept Sammy calmer.

Across the way, Penny's front door opened, and Jack felt an absurd hope that Arianna would come out, even though she didn't use that entrance and her car wasn't there.

Then the hope within him made him angry. It didn't matter if she showed her face; he wasn't going to invite her in for coffee. It wasn't like he was going to let her see Sammy.

And he had the feeling that if Sammy saw her, and wasn't allowed to go to her, the meltdown would be massive.

"Hey, Jack!" Penny's cheerful voice matched the cheerful barking of Buster, Arianna's puppy. "Okay if I bring him over?"

"If he's leashed. Sammy's still a little afraid."

"Sure." She held the pup at the bottom of the steps

while Jack sat at the top, holding Sammy. Sammy reached toward the dog, so Jack scooted down another step, then another. Finally, he and the pup were only a couple of feet apart. "That's about where Arianna stopped," Penny said.

Even the mention of her name made Jack sweat. "What do you mean, she stopped there?"

"Desensitizing Sammy," Penny said. "She's been working to get him used to the puppy ever since she got Buster. Inch by inch, pretty much."

Why did he seem to know less than anyone about his own son?

"I thought you'd be at work," Penny said. "Wasn't Mrs. Jennings's car out here a little while ago?"

Jack explained about the pills. "I have a call in to Sammy's doctor, but I have the feeling we have an answer as to why Sammy got so sick. The information about what kind of drug it was is probably irrelevant by now, but it would've been good to know at the time."

Maybe Arianna wouldn't have been pushed to confess the truth, he thought darkly. Maybe he'd still be a happy idiot.

"Do you need someone to take care of Sammy today?" Penny glanced toward the barn. "I have some work to do, but I could bring him along."

"I canceled my appointments. I can't ask that of you."

She nodded, sitting down on the edge of the steps to rub the puppy's belly. "That's all well and good, but what are you going to do tomorrow?"

"I don't know," he said, sighing.

"Look, why don't you come up to the barn with me? You and Sammy don't need to sit here by yourselves feeling blue."

Jack had a "what does it matter" feeling that was pretty alien to him. "Okay," he said. He'd been fueled by anger since Arianna's big reveal, but it was starting to trickle away. Surging up now and then, yeah, but he just wasn't the angry type.

Instead, hopelessness pressed down on him like storm clouds pressing against the mountains, dark and ominous. Thing was, he'd started to hope for a future brighter than the past. A future where Sammy would thrive and they'd have a warm, happy home. A future where Sammy would have the love and warmth of a mother.

A future where he'd have the heart-filling, joyous, expansive experience of loving and being truly loved.

But that had evaporated with Arianna's stunning words, and now that anger wasn't filling the hole that remained behind, he just felt dry and empty.

Up at the barn, Penny let dogs out of their crates and Jack walked them outside to do their business, carrying Sammy on his shoulders. It was true, Sammy was much more comfortable with dogs now. He guessed he had Arianna to thank for that. Not that he felt the least bit thankful to her.

Willie came in and took charge of Sammy, and once again, Jack was surprised. His son went readily to the rough-voiced older man.

The ranch was good for Sammy.

It was good for Jack, too, because he had close friends, like Penny and Willie, who refused to let him sink into despair. And suddenly, he wanted to know what they thought of the whole wretched situation. "Did Arianna talk to you?" he asked Penny.

She frowned. "I spoke to her briefly last night, when she asked if I could take care of Buster."

Why'd she need that? Where was she staying?

He suppressed the questions he had no business asking, but Penny squinted at him. "She stayed down at Carson and Lily's," she said.

Had she read his mind?

And why was he so relieved that she hadn't slept over at Nathan's or traveled to see him?

"I tried to find out what was going on between the two of you," Penny said with a hint of a smile, "but she said it wasn't her story to tell. Said it was yours."

"Well, it's kind of hers," he said. And then before he could think himself out of it, he blurted out, "She's Sammy's mother."

Penny stared and sucked in a breath. "You're kidding me. And you didn't know?"

He shook his head.

"Chloe?"

"She knew. They kept it from me."

There was a cough behind them. "Sorry, didn't mean to eavesdrop," Willie said. "But no point pretending I didn't overhear. That has a whole lot of ramifications, doesn't it?"

Jack nodded once. "The main one being, I know now I can't trust her."

"That's… Well, I can see why you'd say that, for sure. But she's a good person. This just doesn't sound like her." Penny frowned.

In a strange way, Jack was relieved that Penny thought well of Arianna and was taken aback by what she'd done. Made him feel like less of a fool. "I guess none of us knew her as well as we thought we did."

They all took care of the dogs for a little bit, and finally, all three adults and Sammy ended up in the big field behind the barn, watching the puppy romp with the mother dog and her pup, the ones who'd taken him in.

"Dogs sure know how to be happy," Willie said, chewing on a blade of grass.

Penny gave Jack a meaningful look. "Even if someone kicks them or hits them, they jump right back up, ready to love again. Our rescue program is proof of that."

Was this some kind of heavy-handed lesson they were trying to teach? "I'm not a dog," he said. "My memory's a little longer."

"Believe me, I get it," Penny said, looking out across the horizon.

Jack realized with a jolt how much Penny had had to forgive, her husband having left her for another woman, an alleged friend.

"Did you ever hear how me and Long John got to be such good friends?" Willie asked.

Jack shook his head.

"He sought me out after 'Nam," Willie said. Now he was looking out toward the mountains, too. "He'd been in battle with my twin brother and he wanted to tell me about it."

Jack noticed that Penny put her hand on Willie's back, patting it a little. He was guessing this story wouldn't have a happy ending.

"They were in a firefight together, and Long John just…left him there," Willie said. "Saved himself. Ricky was down—and hurt pretty bad, sure. He probably wouldn't have made it. But…" The older man's eyes welled up, and he swallowed hard, got himself under control. "His remains were never recovered."

Jack blew out a breath. "I'm sorry."

"Me, too. But before I was sorry, I was mad. I knocked Long John plumb out when I heard."

Penny put a hand on Willie's arm. "What made you forgive him?"

He shrugged. "There were a lot of circumstances. He was sorry. He regretted it."

"Still," Penny said, "that must have been hard to do."

"It was," Willie said. "I wanted someone to blame. But when I let go of that, I ended up with the best friend of my life."

Both of the elders looked at Jack.

"You could end up with something good, too, Jack," Penny said softly. "Something that would be good for Sammy, too, because you know it's better for him to know his biological parents than not."

"*Parents.* Plural." Jack heaved a giant sigh. He couldn't imagine opening his heart to Arianna, let alone to Nathan, too.

"First things first," Penny said. "Why don't you talk to Arianna?"

"No, uh-uh. She lied to me."

"She was in an impossible situation, sounds like," Penny said. "She was pregnant and desperate, and she had the chance to have her baby raised within her own family with a stable mother and father, only there was a condition. That's what it sounds like anyway, right?"

Jack nodded. "Chloe apparently made her promise not to tell me or anyone."

"So Chloe is as much to blame as Arianna, right?"

"Was," Jack said. "Yeah. I guess."

They were all silent for a few minutes, watching the puppies frolic. Sammy was actually rolling around with them just like any other little kid, and Jack couldn't help but be warmed by that.

"Would you change anything that happened?" Willie asked finally.

The question stopped Jack short. Would he? If anything changed, he wouldn't have Sammy. "No," he said quietly, "I guess I wouldn't."

"Then it's just possible," Penny said, "that God had a plan."

Jack thought about that as he walked back down to his house, slowly, adjusting to Sammy's pace. He had to admit it was possible.

He just didn't understand what the plan was.

The next morning, Jack woke up with his heart in his shoes. He had to move forward, had to find care for Sammy, had to go to work and keep his appointments. People were depending on him. But he didn't feel like doing anything at all.

He'd spent the night looking out at the stars and thinking. He knew that Penny and Willie had his and Sammy's good at heart. He even knew they were probably right. But his heart was so raw.

Why had Arianna let him kiss her and acted like she was attached? Because she *was* attached, or because she was Sammy's mother?

He was ashamed to admit to himself that he could forgive her more easily if he knew she hadn't been faking her feelings for him.

But if he couldn't tell the difference between fake feelings and real ones, how could he ever succeed at a relationship?

He grabbed his phone and clicked off his "do not

disturb" to start searching for sitters, and a text pinged in. From Arianna. In a moment of weakness, he'd lifted the block on her number.

He didn't want to look at it, was mad when he couldn't resist.

These six sitters are willing to care for Sammy today and for the rest of the week. All experienced and highly recommended.

There was a list with phone numbers he could just click.

Her own name was last on the list.

Jack didn't want to accept help from her, but he did need care for Sammy. He only hesitated a minute before he clicked on the number of a woman who worked in the nursery at church.

He should have thought of her before; Sammy knew her. Soon, he'd arranged care for the rest of Sammy's week.

He should thank Arianna. But she was obviously just trying impress him. He turned off the phone and started packing Sammy's bag for the new sitter.

That night, when he and Sammy got home, there was a casserole on his doorstep with a note. "Pasta with Alfredo sauce and veggies. Microwave 2–3 minutes. Sammy loves it and you might, too. —A"

She needed to leave him alone. She wasn't getting back in his good graces just by providing a babysitter and a meal. In no way did that outweigh the horrible betrayal she'd committed.

He did take the casserole inside and serve it up,

though, because both he and Sammy were starving. They ate almost all of it in one sitting.

She did it all week. A new interactive toy that Sammy adored on sight. A six-pack of Jack's favorite soft drink and two bags of the kind of pretzels he loved but could rarely find around here. A new jacket for Sammy with a note clipped to it: "You should cut out the tags before putting this on him—they're too scratchy for him."

He hated it that she knew more about his child than he did. Hated that her gifts were so perfect.

None of it was going to open the door to his heart.

The next time, he caught her: she was delivering a big portrait of Sammy, laughing. It was in her trademark primitive style, but a perfect likeness for all that.

He flung open the door. "Why can't you just leave us alone?"

She paused in the act of setting down the portrait. "I can't. He's my son, and I'm not abandoning him again."

Sammy had fallen asleep on the floor and Jack didn't want to wake him, but he'd had enough. He was going to have to lay it out for her again. He came out onto the porch and shut the door behind him. "Do you realize how awful it is, what you did?"

She met his eyes steadily. "Yes, I do," she said. "I'm truly sorry, Jack. I made a horrible mistake of judgment."

He waited for the excuses, but they didn't come. She just stood there, watching him.

He *wasn't* going to forgive her.

"I'm hoping one day you'll forgive me," she said, seeming to read his mind, "and let me see Sammy."

"Not happening," he said. "Some things are unforgivable."

He went back inside, slammed the door and didn't feel

nearly as gratified as he should have. Especially since the loud slam woke up Sammy.

Later that night, his father called. Of course, he'd heard that Jack had missed a couple days of work. More disturbing, he wanted to know if the rumors around town were true.

Someone at the hospital must have overheard Jack and Arianna talking, or read a notation in Sammy's chart. Or maybe Arianna had told one of her friends who'd spread the word. It didn't matter; there was no point hiding something that would soon come out anyway, so Jack confirmed the rumors. "It's true, Dad. Arianna is Sammy's biological mother."

They talked for a few minutes, Dad sputtering and angry. "Some things are unforgivable," he said as he hung up.

The words sent a sharp chill through Jack.

He'd said those exact same words to Arianna just a few hours ago.

Was he turning into his father?

"Am I, God?" he demanded, looking upward.

He seemed to sense God chuckling, telling him it was his choice. Jack had free will: he could turn into his father, or not.

He thought about what Willie and Penny had said: that Arianna had faced an awful and impossible decision.

It was hard for Jack to put himself in her shoes—he was a man after all, and would never bear a child—but he did know something about putting his own feelings aside for the good of his son.

If she had done it, he could do it, too. Before he could

lose his nerve, before his usual nonspontaneous habits could kick in, he texted her. Can you come over?

He'd envisioned a quiet talk, a start toward forgiveness, but when Arianna came in, Sammy woke up again. Her look at him was stark, hungry, but she turned her eyes toward Jack and didn't go to Sammy.

Sammy saw her and his eyes widened. "Ah-ah. Aunt Ah-ah." He held out his arms toward her.

They were clear words, and the first he'd spoken since way before his diagnosis.

Arianna put a hand to her mouth, tears filling her eyes. "Oh, Jack." She glanced over at him and then back at Sammy. "Oh, sweetheart, come here. Is that okay?" she added, looking at Jack.

Jack nodded because he couldn't speak through the lump in his throat.

She held out her arms.

"Aunt Ah-ah!" Sammy toddled toward her.

She clasped Sammy in her arms.

Jack watched the two of them and wondered how he hadn't noticed that the glints in Sammy's hair were the same color as those in Arianna's. Even more, how could he have missed the loving, completely maternal way she held him?

He was in danger of breaking down and sobbing, especially as the significance of Sammy's speech dawned on him. If he could say two words, he could learn many more. If he could speak, he could communicate.

And he'd communicated out of caring for Arianna. Which was contrary to all the stereotypes about autism. Sammy had feelings, deep and loyal.

Arianna was unlocking them.

She'd unlocked Jack's heart, as well. He'd doubted

his ability to have a relationship, doubted that anyone would care for him. But in word and action, Arianna had shown that she cared. For Sammy, yes, of course.

But she seemed to care for him, too, and he almost couldn't breathe with the joy of it.

Almost couldn't believe it, either. Maybe the texts and the babysitter list and the casserole were all for Sammy, all so that she could see her son. Maybe she cared nothing for Jack; maybe he was a means to an end.

Sammy struggled free of her arms and she let him go, making sure he was steady on his feet before releasing him. He toddled straight to Jack and made the sign for "father."

"Da!" he said. "Da!"

Jack did break down then. He scooped Sammy into his arms and buried his face in his son's sweaty hair and let himself cry a little.

All the emotions and hugging were too much for Sammy, of course. He wriggled free and crawled to his bear and flung himself down on it, rubbing the backs of his hands over his eyes.

Jack got control of himself and then passed the tissue box over to Arianna, and a few minutes later they put Sammy to bed.

"Thank you so much for letting me see him," Arianna said as they came back downstairs. "I know it's hard for you and I won't abuse the privilege."

Jack waited until she was down the steps and standing beside him. He smiled at her. "You can see him whenever you want."

Her eyes lit up. "Thank you!"

She was *so* beautiful.

They stood looking at each other, beaming, really,

until a cloud flickered across Arianna's eyes. She shook her head a little and turned away. "Thank you again, Jack. I guess I should go."

"Arianna."

She paused in the act of picking up her purse.

"Do you want to go?"

"No." Her head was bowed. She didn't look at him.

"Why not?" Maybe it was cruel of him, but he wasn't content with guessing about her feelings. He knew his own—he'd realized them for sure when he'd seen her holding Sammy—but hers were still a mystery.

She drew in a breath, put down her purse and turned to face him, meeting his eyes. "I miss what we had, Jack, or what we were starting to have. Independent of Sammy."

Her warm words seemed to permeate his very core. She missed *him*.

"I've missed you, too," he admitted.

She reached out and put her arms around him in a hug that felt like nourishment after starvation. Neither of them let go for a long time.

Finally, he broke their embrace, took a step back and put his hands on her shoulders. "I'm sorry I've been so harsh and judgmental. I guess… I guess I was hurt, but that's no excuse."

She shook her head rapidly and reached out to put a finger on his lips. "There's no need to apologize. What you did was nothing compared to what I did, and I'll never stop being sorry for it."

"Ah." He cupped her face in his hands. "No, Arianna. Don't let guilt get in the way of something beautiful."

"What's that?" She was staring at him, eyes glittering with unshed tears.

"These feelings between us. I love you, Arianna," he said.

She bit her lip, a tear spilling out.

He wiped it away with his thumb. "I think it started when you came in here with that crazy sunflower picture." He nodded toward it, now proudly displayed over the couch that it most definitely didn't match.

She laughed a little. "Even though I made a mess of your house?"

"You brought in color and warmth and life. For both of us. I..." He drew in a breath, trying to phrase it right. "You've been helping both me and Sammy to heal, and I love you for it. And I love you for your creativity and your energy and your sense of fun. The way you care about other people and know just what to do to help them. The way you've helped your aunt and uncle clean up their house, and the way you've been training that puppy to be careful around Sammy."

A dimple quirked in her cheek, and she pulled away, her cheeks going pink. "You noticed."

"I think I notice everything about you," he admitted. "But I still wonder...how do you feel about me, Arianna? Can we...pursue this?"

She looked up at him through her lashes and brushed a stray curl back from her face. "I think...I love you, too."

"You think so?"

She nodded, smiling.

Jack's heart pounded like the hooves of a racehorse. He reached for her.

She held up a hand. "Wait," she said seriously. "There's something I want you to know."

He took her hand and tugged her to sit beside him

on the couch, right underneath the sunflower painting. "You can tell me anything."

"I won't keep anything from you ever again." She clutched his hand tighter and looked into his eyes. "That's why... I know how it looks, the fact that I got pregnant out of wedlock. But that was a mistake I won't make again. I intend to wait for when, or if, I get married."

He looked at her, and love for the strong woman she was, for her values and her goodness, her ability to make a new start, seemed to fill his heart. "If I have anything to do with it," he said, his voice catching, "you won't be waiting long at all."

Epilogue

Eighteen months later

Balloons were flying at the entrance to the newly renovated Redemption Ranch lodge as Arianna, Jack and Sammy walked into the warm, welcoming great room. Arianna looked over at Sammy, worried he wouldn't like the colorful change to a familiar environment. And indeed, he studied the balloons impassively for a moment.

"Balloons, Sammy. How do you like the balloons?"

He studied them for a moment longer. "'Loons," he said and nodded once. The shadow of a smile crossed his three-year-old face. "Like 'loons."

She swept him up in a hug. "Good words!"

"You little pistol." Jack tickled Sammy's chin, making him giggle. "You knew you'd get a hug from Mommy for that."

Arianna still got a warm, happy feeling when she heard her husband refer to her as Sammy's mommy, because there was no ambivalence or discomfort in his tone. With God's help, they'd worked through it and it wasn't a barrier to their happy marriage. Their *very* happy marriage. She leaned into him, and he put an arm around her.

All their friends were here: Gabe and Daniela with their baby, named Tommy for one of Gabe's fallen comrades, and Lily and Carson and the twins, Sunny and Skye, who had been so wonderful helping Arianna and Jack manage the hard time they'd gone through.

Finn and Kayla were here with Leo, now a big third grader. And of course, Penny, Long John and his wife, and Willie. And Branson Howe, the banker, which was a little bit surprising.

After everyone had eaten a kid-friendly meal of pizza and pasta, and the kids were playing with Sammy's toys—he had plenty, and no problem at all sharing his wealth—Penny gestured to bring the adults together. "I love you guys so much," she said. "And I want you to be the first to know that, thanks to our donors, including many of you, we're burning up the mortgage to Redemption Ranch, because it's all paid off."

The door opened, and everyone turned as Nathan came rushing in. "Sorry to be late," he said. "I didn't... Well, I appreciate the invitation." His eyes scanned the children, and his small smile told Arianna he'd found Sammy at the center of the kids.

"We're glad you came, too," Penny said to Nathan, "because your donation is the one that put us over the top in paying off the ranch."

Arianna lifted an eyebrow and looked over at Jack. His eyes had narrowed a little, and he looked surprised and interested, but not angry.

He was the best husband in the world.

"As long as we're making announcements," Willie said, "Penny and I have one, too."

Arianna sucked in a breath and looked at Penny.

She was smiling at Willie with eyes full of love.

Willie cleared his throat. "She and I, well, we're going to get married."

There was general cheering and hugging, and Arianna's heart was full. So much to celebrate, and these people were all so dear to her. She and Jack and Sammy were richly blessed.

Jack walked Branson Howe to the door. "You okay, man?" he asked.

"Yeah. I wish them well." He took one more glance back at the room, where people were toasting Penny and Willie, and shook his head. "Next time, if there is one, I'll try harder."

"There will be," Jack said. Sometime in the past year, he'd become an optimist about the future.

Jack looked across the room to where Nathan knelt in front of Sammy. They were both engrossed with a complicated and undoubtedly very expensive truck that Nathan had brought for Sammy's birthday.

They didn't look much alike, but the intensity they shared, their complete focus on what was in front of them rather than the din of the party around them, identified them, at least to Jack, as father and son.

It's good for Sammy.

Of course, Sammy was too young to understand about biological parents. They had started telling him a simplified version of his adoption story, but for now, he didn't have much interest.

As Jack watched, Arianna turned from refilling drinks and walked over toward Nathan and Sammy. She squatted down to admire the truck with them.

Emotion flashed through Jack, jealousy and longing, but it was clean now. He wasn't ashamed of how he felt, and that helped him be in control of it. He drew in a couple of deep, calming breaths and walked over to the trio.

"Daddy!" Sammy held up his arms, and Jack reached down to pick him up, his heart swelling with love. Nathan stood then, too. He met Jack's eyes and gave a little nod, and Jack understood.

It was a thank-you. Nathan was grateful to be involved in Sammy's life. And Jack knew that as time went on, that involvement might become greater. Nathan might be a huge resource to Sammy, and that would be a good thing. Jack felt big enough to let it happen now.

"Bus! Bus!" Sammy struggled to get down as Buster, now a full-grown retriever mix, let out one deep bark. Sammy wrapped his arms around the dog's neck for a none-too-gentle hug, which Buster endured patiently. Then the two of them headed off toward the other children.

Arianna slid an arm around Jack, and when he looked down at her, her eyes were warm with love. He tugged her closer, putting an arm around her slender waist and letting him his fingers stretch to touch her slightly convex abdomen. "You're sure we can't tell everyone tonight? Today?"

"It's only four months. I still feel like it's too early." She smiled at him and relented. "Pretty soon, I'll let you shout it from the rooftops."

And that, he reflected as gratitude flooded his heart, he would certainly do.

* * * * *

*Don't miss these other books in
Lee Tobin McClain's
Redemption Ranch miniseries:*

The Soldier's Redemption
The Twins' Family Christmas

Available now from Love Inspired!

*Find more great reads at
www.LoveInspired.com.*

Dear Reader,

This third book in the Redemption Ranch series is special to me, because it's about how we can be free to be our perfectly imperfect selves. Arianna feels shame about mistakes she made in the past; that sense of inadequacy, plus a promise she made to her sister, pushes her to keep a secret that should never have been. As for Jack, he believes he's too staid and dull for a colorful, flamboyant woman like Arianna. The reality is that both of them are just as God made them to be, their mistakes can be forgiven…and they're perfect for one another. How wonderful!

The cream-colored puppy, Buster, who shows up on Arianna's doorstep has a real-life model: my own golden doodle, Nash. If you enjoyed Buster, visit @nash_the_goldendoodle's Instagram account to keep up with a lot of dog shenanigans.

Thank you for reading, and may God's blessings follow you wherever you go.

Lee

COMING NEXT MONTH FROM
Love Inspired®

Available August 19, 2019

SHELTER FROM THE STORM
North Country Amish • by Patricia Davids
Pregnant and unwed, Gemma Lapp's determined to return to her former home in Maine. After she misses her bus, the only way to get there is riding with her former crush, Jesse Crump. And when he learns her secret, he might just have a proposal that'll solve all her problems...

HER FORGOTTEN COWBOY
Cowboy Country • by Deb Kastner
After a car accident leaves Rebecca Hamilton with amnesia, the best way to recover her memory is by moving back to her ranch—with her estranged husband, whose unborn child she carries. As she rediscovers herself, can Rebecca and Tanner also reclaim their love and marriage?

THE BULL RIDER'S SECRET
Colorado Grooms • by Jill Lynn
Mackenzie Wilder isn't happy when her brother hires her ex-boyfriend, Jace Hawke, to help out on their family's guest ranch for the summer. Jace broke her heart when he left town without an explanation. But can he convince her he deserves a second chance?

REUNITED IN THE ROCKIES
Rocky Mountain Heroes • by Mindy Obenhaus
Stopping to help a pregnant stranded driver, police officer Jude Stephens comes face-to-face with the last person he expected—the woman he once loved. Now with both of them working on a local hotel's renovations, can Jude and Kayla Bradshaw overcome their past to build a future together?

A MOTHER FOR HIS TWINS
by Jill Weatherholt
First-grade teacher Joy Kelliher has two new students—twin little boys who belong to her high school sweetheart. And if teaching Nick Capello's sons wasn't enough, the widower's also her neighbor...and competing for the principal job she wants. Will little matchmakers bring about a reunion Joy never anticipated?

HOMETOWN HEALING
by Jennifer Slattery
Returning home with a baby in tow, Paige Cordell's determined her stay is only temporary. But to earn enough money to leave, she needs a job—and her only option is working at her first love's dinner theater. Now can Jed Gilbertson convince her to stay for good? _____

LOOK FOR THESE AND OTHER LOVE INSPIRED BOOKS WHEREVER BOOKS ARE SOLD, INCLUDING MOST BOOKSTORES, SUPERMARKETS, DISCOUNT STORES AND DRUGSTORES.

LICNM0819

Get 4 FREE REWARDS!

We'll send you 2 FREE Books plus 2 FREE Mystery Gifts.

His Wyoming Baby Blessing
Jill Kemerer

Her Twins' Cowboy Dad
Patricia Johns

Love Inspired® books feature contemporary inspirational romances with Christian characters facing the challenges of life and love.

FREE
Value Over
$20

YES! Please send me 2 FREE Love Inspired® Romance novels and my 2 FREE mystery gifts (gifts are worth about $10 retail). After receiving them, if I don't wish to receive any more books, I can return the shipping statement marked "cancel." If I don't cancel, I will receive 6 brand-new novels every month and be billed just $5.24 for the regular-print edition or $5.99 each for the larger-print edition in the U.S., or $5.74 each for the regular-print edition or $6.24 each for the larger-print edition in Canada. That's a savings of at least 13% off the cover price. It's quite a bargain! Shipping and handling is just 50¢ per book in the U.S. and $1.25 per book in Canada.* I understand that accepting the 2 free books and gifts places me under no obligation to buy anything. I can always return a shipment and cancel at any time. The free books and gifts are mine to keep no matter what I decide.

Choose one:
☐ **Love Inspired® Romance Regular-Print**
(105/305 IDN GNWC)

☐ **Love Inspired® Romance Larger-Print**
(122/322 IDN GNWC)

Name (please print)

Address   Apt. #

City   State/Province   Zip/Postal Code

Mail to the **Reader Service:**
IN U.S.A.: P.O. Box 1341, Buffalo, NY 14240-8531
IN CANADA: P.O. Box 603, Fort Erie, Ontario L2A 5X3

Want to try 2 free books from another series? Call 1-800-873-8635 or visit www.ReaderService.com.

---

*Terms and prices subject to change without notice. Prices do not include sales taxes, which will be charged (if applicable) based on your state or country of residence. Canadian residents will be charged applicable taxes. Offer not valid in Quebec. This offer is limited to one order per household. Books received may not be as shown. Not valid for current subscribers to Love Inspired Romance books. All orders subject to approval. Credit or debit balances in a customer's account(s) may be offset by any other outstanding balance owed by or to the customer. Please allow 4 to 6 weeks for delivery. Offer available while quantities last.

Your Privacy—The Reader Service is committed to protecting your privacy. Our Privacy Policy is available online at www.ReaderService.com or upon request from the Reader Service. We make a portion of our mailing list available to reputable third parties that offer products we believe may interest you. If you prefer that we not exchange your name with third parties, or if you wish to clarify or modify your communication preferences, please visit us at www.ReaderService.com/consumerschoice or write to us at Reader Service Preference Service, P.O. Box 9062, Buffalo, NY 14240-9062. Include your complete name and address.

LI19R3

Return to Safe Haven, where a new beginning with your first love is only a heartbeat away...

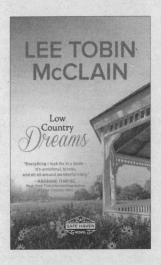

"*Low Country Hero* has everything I look for in a book—it's emotional, tender, and an all-around wonderful story."
—*New York Times* bestselling author RaeAnne Thayne

Be sure to connect with us at:

Harlequin.com/Newsletters
Facebook.com/HarlequinBooks
Twitter.com/HQNBooks

HQN™

HQNBooks.com

PHLTM0619BPA

SPECIAL EXCERPT FROM

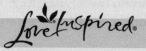

*On her way home, pregnant and alone,
an Amish woman finds herself stranded
with the last person she wanted to see.*

Read on for a sneak preview of
Shelter from the Storm *by Patricia Davids,
available September 2019 from Love Inspired.*

"There won't be another bus going that way until the day after tomorrow."

"Are you sure?" Gemma Lapp stared at the agent behind the counter in stunned disbelief.

"Of course I'm sure. I work for the bus company."

She clasped her hands together tightly, praying the tears that pricked the backs of her eyes wouldn't start flowing. She couldn't afford a motel room for two nights.

She wheeled her suitcase over to the bench. Sitting down with a sigh, she moved her suitcase in front of her so she could prop up her swollen feet. After two solid days on a bus she was ready to lie down. Anywhere.

She bit her lower lip to stop it from quivering. She could place a call to the phone shack her parents shared with their Amish neighbors to let them know she was returning and ask her father to send a car for her, but she would have to leave a message.

Any message she left would be overheard. If she gave the real reason, even Jesse Crump would know before she reached home. She couldn't bear that, although she didn't understand why his opinion mattered so much. His stoic face wouldn't reveal his thoughts, but he was sure to gloat when he learned he'd been right about her reckless ways. He had said she was looking for trouble and that she would find it sooner or later. Well, she had found it all right.

No, she wouldn't call. What she had to say was better said face-to-face. She was cowardly enough to delay as long as possible.

She didn't know how she was going to find the courage to tell her mother and father that she was six months pregnant, and Robert Troyer, the man who'd promised to marry her, was long gone.

Don't miss
Shelter from the Storm *by* USA TODAY
bestselling author Patricia Davids,
available September 2019 wherever
Love Inspired® books and ebooks are sold.

www.LoveInspired.com

Copyright © 2019 by Patricia MacDonald

LIEXP0819

Looking for inspiration in tales
of hope, faith and heartfelt romance?

Check out **Love Inspired**® and
Love Inspired® **Suspense** books!

New books available every month!

CONNECT WITH US AT:

Facebook.com/groups/HarlequinConnection

 Facebook.com/HarlequinBooks

 Twitter.com/HarlequinBooks

 Instagram.com/HarlequinBooks

 Pinterest.com/HarlequinBooks

ReaderService.com

Love Inspired®

LIGENRE2018R2